A
Good
Kind of
Trouble

Lisa Moore Ramée

Balzer + Bray

An Imprint of HarperCollins*Publishers*

Balzer + Bray is an imprint of HarperCollins Publishers.

A Good Kind of Trouble
Copyright © 2019 by Lisa Moore Ramée
Emoji icons provided by EmojiOne
address HarperCollins Children's Books, a division of HarperCollins
Publishers, 195 Broadway, New York, NY 10007.
www.harpercollinschildrens.com

ISBN 978-0-06-283668-7

Typography Aurora Parlagreco
20 21 22 23   PC/LSCH   10

First Edition

For Morgan,
More, always and forever

1
First Slide

I'm allergic to trouble. It makes my hands itch. But today in science, when Mr. Levy starts calling out lab-partner assignments, I don't get even the lightest tingle. I just sit there, barely breathing, waiting for him to assign me to the perfect partner. He's been promising we'd start science labs since the first day of school, but it's been *weeks*. Lots of time for me to decide on the perfect partner.

Mr. Levy has been teaching science at Emerson Junior High for centuries, and he looks like a mad scientist. For real. He has wild, frizzy gray hair and even wears a lab coat every day.

He fluffs his hair and adjusts his thick black glasses. I start rubbing my hands against my legs, which isn't a good sign, but I don't pay attention. Any second he will get to my name.

"Shayla and . . ." Mr. Levy pauses a few seconds, like he is really thinking about it. Like he doesn't already have the list in front of him. "And Bernard," he says.

No. And I mean, *no*. This is the opposite of perfect.

I sneak a peek behind me. Bernard sits in the back, slouching low in his seat. Junior-high desks weren't made for Bernard. He's not kid sized. He's grown-up sized. And grown-up *big*.

He catches me looking at him, and his mouth shifts into a mean grimace. I gulp and look away.

My sister, Hana, would say I'm being just like *those people* who take one look at a Black person and think they need to clutch their purse tight or lock their car doors. I have no problem with Bernard being Black. *Obviously.* I'm Black too. It's him being huge and mean and scary.

Bernard went to the same elementary school as me and my best friends, Isabella and Julia. We're all terrified of him. Everyone I *know* is terrified of him. Even in kindergarten he would scowl at everybody. And he'd yell. A *lot*.

In second grade he yelled at me because I got to the *Star Wars* Legos before he did. He grabbed those storm-troopers right out of my hands, and if you've ever had someone snatch Legos from you, you know how much it hurts. And he didn't say sorry.

I told him I *needed* the stormtroopers. But Bernard looked at me like he wouldn't have minded squashing me right underneath one of his big shoes.

Bernard was a bully then, and he's a bully now.

Please, oh, please don't let us be doing lab work today.

"Find your partners, everyone!" Mr. Levy claps his hands together. I just bet partnering me with Bernard is some devious experiment: what happens if we mix trouble-hating girl with bully boy?

Kaboom. That's what.

"Shayla!" Bernard hollers.

He sounds mad. I guess he's not happy that we're partners either.

I walk to the back of the room to the lab tables, and my feet feel like they weigh six hundred pounds.

"I got the first slide!" Bernard's voice is like a bunch of bowling balls all being dropped at the same time. The glass in one of his big paws snaps in two.

"Oh," I say. He could probably snap one of my fingers just like that.

Bernard shakes his hand and starts sucking a finger.

I'm sure that is a bad idea. Mr. Levy comes over and sets some new slides next to our microscope. He doesn't even ask Bernard if he's okay.

Bernard doesn't look okay; he looks angry, which is basically saying he looks like Bernard.

"Stop messing around," Mr. Levy tells Bernard.

"I wasn't!" Bernard booms.

Mr. Levy shakes his head and walks away.

After that, Bernard won't even look in the microscope. He shoves the stack of slides at me, like it's *my* fault he broke the first one.

The top slide has a tiny green-brown thing on it, and when I peer through the microscope, I can see it's a bug leg. I think it's from a grasshopper and write some notes about it and try *not* to study Bernard. I don't know if I should say anything to him. I don't want to make him even more mad.

When class is over, he gets up so fast, he knocks his desk to its side, and instead of picking it up, he storms out of the room.

You bet Mr. Levy frowns real hard at that.

I pick up Bernard's desk before leaving class. Maybe since Mr. Levy didn't have to pick it up, no one will get in trouble, but my hands itch anyway.

2
Triangle Friends

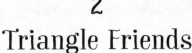

We have a break right after second period, and it's the first time of the day when I can meet up with Isabella and Julia. When we got our schedules on Maze Day, we couldn't believe out of six classes we didn't have one together. How is that even possible? I'm only in pre-algebra, but I'm pretty sure the odds of that have got to be crazy high.

Only getting to see my friends at break and lunch is the worst.

Some people think it's weird I have two best friends. "But who's your *favorite*?" they'll ask.

Who could pick between pizza and spaghetti? They're both the best.

We make a great triangle. And three is actually a magic number. I learned that from the Schoolhouse Rock! DVDs.

We are alike in everything that matters. We call ourselves the United Nations, because Isabella is Puerto Rican and Julia is Japanese American, and then there's me—and yes, we know Black isn't a nation, but we also know we are *united*.

We've been friends since forever, but super *best* friends since third grade, when we got partnered for a group project. Each group was assigned a place in the world and then had to give a presentation like we were tour guides. We got Hawaii, and Momma bought fake palm trees and coconuts from Dollar Tree, and Isabella's mom, who's a graphic designer, helped us make travel brochures. Isabella painted an amazing poster of a Hawaiian beach at sunset. Julia was really excited because she has a lot of family living in Hawaii. She brought in a whole bunch of shell necklaces and postcards and even a bottle full of sand from a Hawaiian beach.

We've been united ever since.

Every day at break, we meet behind the row of extra classrooms next to the multipurpose room. Even though the buildings are called portables, I don't think they ever get moved once they're set down.

Isabella is already there, claiming our spot, right

under the huge magnolia tree. But there's no sign of Julia yet. Isabella's T-shirt is a swirl of peach and rose with a hint of pale blue. It looks like a dawn sky. It is beautiful, and I'm immediately jealous.

"That is the cutest top, Is," I say. "When did you get it?"

Isabella looks down at herself as if she can't remember what she's wearing. "It's just tie-dye." She stretches the material out, examining the colors. "I was trying for a sort of ombré thing. It didn't work exactly."

"You *made* it?" I am as close to squealing as I get.

She shrugs. "It was easy. You just have to be careful how you tie the rubber bands."

"Well, next time we do a tie-dye project, you're totally making mine," I say.

"You got it," Isabella says with a smile.

"Where's Jules?" I ask. I can't wait to share my horrible science-lab news, but I can't say anything until it's the three of us.

Isabella points, and I turn to see Julia running toward us.

When she reaches us, she's all out of breath and plops down next to me and Isabella. She digs an apple out of her backpack. "Sorry I'm late. Mr. Lee took forever handing back homework."

"What did you get?" I ask, and Julia frowns at me. Grades aren't her thing the way they are mine. I mean, she does fine; she just doesn't care.

We all stretch out our legs: my long, skinny, dark brown ones next to Isabella's tan ones, next to Julia's much lighter ones. We're all wearing low-top black Converses. Julia's are really worn out, and Isabella's are splotched with purple paint. Mine look like they just came out of the box—I like things neat.

Since break is only twelve minutes, we don't have time to waste, and we're already starting late, so I blurt out, "You'll never guess who my lab partner is." It's funny how even terrible news can be exciting to tell.

"Not that jerk who talked about your forehead?" Julia asks, and takes a huge bite of her apple.

I put a hand over my forehead. On the very first day, in my very first class, there he was. Jace Hayward, with his cinnamon skin that's just a little lighter than mine, and those wide, lime-green eyes, and a grin as cool as lake water. I had told Julia and Isabella that this was the year I was going to have a boyfriend, and when I saw

Jace, I decided he was the one. If we had gotten partnered today, that would've been the first step. I probably shouldn't have told Julia and Isabella what Jace said about my forehead.

"Jace is not a jerk," I say. "He was just being funny." Although it didn't feel very funny at the time. He called me Jimmy Neutron, and if you've seen that old movie, you know calling me that wasn't any kind of a compliment. Jace said it pretty loud and it made me feel like I swallowed a piece of coal—*while* it was burning. It's true I have a really big forehead. There is exactly four inches of space between my eyebrows and my hairline. I know it's four inches because I measured it one day after hearing someone call me five-head. If you don't think four inches is a lot, go get a ruler and measure your own forehead. I bet you get a two, possibly a three. If you hit a four, hey, I feel you. But I am more than my forehead. Jace just needs to find that out.

Isabella holds up her fists like she might punch somebody. "If he's mean to you again, we'll get him." She tightens her lips over her braces, trying to look tough, but she looks ridiculous. Isabella doesn't have a tough bone in her body.

"Thanks, Is," I say. "I'll definitely knock on *your* door if someone messes with me." That makes me think of Bernard. He broke those slides like they were nothing.

"I hate when people are mean," Isabella says, and grabs some of my baby carrots.

"He wasn't being *mean*, Is," Julia says, and laughs. "He was just being *funny*. Know what I'm saying?"

"Of course, we know what you're saying, Jules," I say, nudging her with my shoulder.

She raises her eyebrow at me. "You're not supposed to say that after."

"Say what?" I ask.

"When someone says, *Know what I'm saying?* it's not like a real question," Julia explains. "It's an expression."

Isabella taps me with a carrot. "Are you going to tell us who your lab partner is or not?" she asks.

"Bernard." I make my voice go really low. "He went *off* in class today. Breaking stuff and knocking his desk over."

"You have to change lab partners!" Isabella squeals.

"I *know*," I say, eyes widening.

"Well, you're doomed," Julia says matter-of-factly,

like she's all ready for my funeral.

"Real helpful, Jules," Isabella says, shaking her head at Julia, then looks at me. "Maybe Mr. Levy will change partners for each lab."

"But what if I'm stuck with him?" I ask.

"You said you wanted a boyfriend," Julia says, and then she busts up laughing.

"You are not even close to funny, Jules." Normally I don't mind Julia's jokes, but Bernard being my boyfriend? That's as funny as lima beans.

Isabella points a carrot at me. "It'll be okay. He can't kill you right in the middle of class."

For some reason that's not nearly as comforting as I want it to be. "You have carrots stuck in your braces," I tell her.

She puts her hand over her mouth. "That's funny because—" Her big hazel eyes get even wider than normal.

"Because what?" I ask.

And then the bell rings, and break's over.

"Gotta go!" Isabella jumps up. Her third period is way on the other side of the school, so she always dashes as soon as the bell rings. "I won't see you guys at lunch," she yells over her shoulder. "I have an appointment." And then she runs off.

"Wait, what?" I call after her, but she doesn't turn back to answer. "Did you know she was leaving school early?" I ask Julia.

"Nope," Julia says. "Hey, don't worry about Bernard."

I hold out my hands so Julia can help me up. "And now I have to go to PE," I groan.

Julia yanks me up from the ground, and for just a tiny second I can imagine flying right over the row of portables and far, far away from PE.

3
Four Laps

It's not that I hate doing anything active, but in elementary school, PE meant going out on the blacktop in your regular clothes and playing softball or capture the flag. It's a whole different bag of chips in junior high.

You have to wear extremely ugly PE clothes that I am positive someone made just to make sure I would look extra bad. Shiny, bright blue shorts are not a good look for me, especially since I had to get a size small on account of me being so skinny. No one wants their shorts falling down. But small shorts are a weird length on me. Too short for baggie basketball, and too long for regular shorts.

And we have to change into our PE clothes right in front of everyone on our row in the locker room. I figured out right away that the best strategy is to change quick so no one gets a good look at anything. What if my underwear is ripped? What if everybody stares at the tiny pimples on my back?

There should really be a law against making kids who are going through puberty undress in public. There should also be a law against going through puberty early. Momma says it's totally normal for a Black girl to start earlier with stuff like *developing* and getting her period and having "grown-up bumps." That's what she calls them, instead of pimples or acne, like that's supposed to make me glad to get them. I don't care if it's normal; I'm not happy about any of it.

In the locker room, the lockers are in long rows, and there are aisles in between with little benches so it's easier to change your shoes. I don't know any of the girls on my aisle, and we all try to keep our eyes on our locker or on the floor. At least that's what I'm hoping they're doing. A girl next to me starts getting undressed, and I do a good job of not noticing her pretty panties with lace and her tiny bra with lots of little hearts. (I wore two shirts in fourth grade before Momma figured it out and bought me a training bra. By fifth grade, I guess I had successfully passed training, because Momma bought me a "real" bra and then new ones in sixth when I went up a size.) My bras are not tiny, or cute. They're big and white and practical.

Yolanda is waiting for me just outside the locker-room doors. Her two front teeth are chipped, making a small upside-down Y in her smile. It makes it easy to remember her name.

We got assigned to be partners for sit-ups on the first day, and now we just partner up all the time. I'm glad about that, because I don't know anyone else in my class. She's in my sixth period too, so it's nice we're sort of becoming friends.

I still haven't gotten used to how much bigger junior high is than elementary school, and how you can be in a class with thirty other kids and not know any of them.

Five different elementary schools feed into Emerson, so there are lots more people.

"Hi." Yolanda flashes a tiny upside-down-Y smile.

"Hi," I say back. Every day I try to guess how Yolanda will be wearing her hair, and I'm usually wrong. She almost always parts it all the way down the middle, making two even sections, but then she'll do something different with the sections. Sometimes she braids them (and sometimes it's one braid, or sometimes it's four, or six). Sometimes the two sections are in big fat curls, and sometimes she connects them together in the back. Once it was two afro puffs.

My English teacher, Ms. Jacobs, assigned a journal project on the first day of school. We're supposed to write all our observations in it. She calls it our eyeball journal because Ralph Waldo Emerson—the person our school is named for—once said he wanted to be an eyeball. I think that sounds gross.

One of the things I always write about is what I observed about Yolanda's hair.

Today she has one tiny braid on each side, and the rest in small curls. "Cute hair," I tell her.

Yolanda puts her hand over her mouth, but I can tell she's got a big grin going. If she wasn't so brown skinned, I bet I would see a blush steaming up her cheeks.

I hear a loud whistle, and our PE teacher, Coach West, shouts, "Hustle on over!"

We hustle and take our places on the hash marks on the ground so Coach West can take roll. My PE shorts rise up when I sit down. I pull at them as if I could make them magically grow longer.

After roll call and stretches, Coach West yells, "Four laps, everybody!" and blows her whistle to get us going. (She really likes her whistle.)

Four laps around the track equals a mile. In junior high, we run a mile every week and we're supposed to get faster each time. Logically, there has to be a point when this is physically impossible, but Coach West doesn't seem to think so.

Our track is made out of recycled tires, so it's easier to run on than asphalt. In the middle of the track is our field that should be green grass but is brown because of the drought. The air is heavy, pressing against me, trying to slow me down.

Yolanda keeps up with me for the first two laps, but by the third one she just waves me ahead.

"Go ahead," she gasps, gripping her side.

This is awkward.

Should I slow down to stay with her? Would it be mean to leave her gasping alone? How would a friendship manual answer these types of questions?

I've never had a Black friend before. My sister makes a huge issue out of that, like there's something wrong with me, but I don't get why it's a big deal. There were hardly any other Black students at my elementary school, and besides, I had Isabella and Julia. Still, I like Yolanda, and even though we're not quite friends yet, we are friendly and I don't want to mess it up.

Coach West blows her whistle again, and I for sure don't want to get in trouble, so I give Yolanda a little wave and keep running.

I'm surprised by how good it feels to run. It's like whatever is circling around in my head bugging me just flies out in the wind and gets left behind on the track. Bye-bye, Bernard! So long, big forehead!

Half a lap ahead of me, I can see this girl Carmetta. She's faster than lightning, and all of a sudden I get this wild idea that maybe I can catch her, so I put on the jets and start running as fast as I can. My heart feels like it's creeping up into my throat, and a pain kicks me right in my side, but I don't stop running.

I don't even come close to catching Carmetta, but when I finish my mile, Coach West clicks her stopwatch and holds her hand up for me to give her a high five. Smacking my hand against hers makes me feel pretty good.

Yolanda doesn't get a high five from Coach. I really don't think she likes running very much. We both head to the water fountain, and I'm wondering if putting deodorant on sweaty pits will keep me from being funky later, when Coach West walks over. "Shayla, you might not know this, but I'm the track coach. You have a nice form going. I think I could use you. Do you want to join the team?"

I rub my hands together because my palms itch all over. "Track?" I ask.

Coach West nods.

"Me?" I glance over at Yolanda and she gives me a little shrug, but she also smiles, so I think she's okay with Coach West not asking her to join the track team.

"Yep!" Coach West grins at me, waiting for an answer.

I want to say no. But Coach West's smile glides over me like sweet syrup and makes my head go up and down. "Great!" she tells me, and blows her whistle. "All right, everybody, I'll see you tomorrow!"

Yolanda elbows me. "Cool," she whispers, making little panting breaths into my ear.

I am positive that track will be many things, but *cool* isn't one of them.

You know what it *does* sound like? A whole steaming plate of trouble.

4
Emerson

Having English after PE is awful because Ms. Jacobs is tough and she hates tardies. So I have to change real quick back into my regular clothes, and I don't even have a second to check a mirror to make sure I'm not looking a mess before flying to room 218. I've only been late once, and Ms. Jacobs gave me a big frown and said not to let it happen again. You bet I haven't.

I'm so busy worrying that I might stink from PE, and thinking about the potential awfulness of being on the track team, that I don't even hear Ms. Jacobs ask her question the first time.

Ms. Jacobs uncaps a blue dry-erase marker, presses the tip to the whiteboard, and looks at the class over her shoulder. "I *asked*, what did everyone find out about Ralph Waldo Emerson last night?"

No one raises their hand, and Ms. Jacobs snaps the

top back onto the marker and faces us. *Uh-oh*. I start rolling my pencil back and forth between my hands to get them to stop itching.

"Isn't there *anyone* who can tell me something about him?" Her exasperated voice has become full-on irritated. She beats her hand with the marker, and each tap hits one of her rings. *Tap, tap, tap*. It's like the ticking of a bomb.

I don't want to see Ms. Jacobs explode. That tight bun of hers would just fly right off her head. "He lived over a hundred years ago," I say. "And he wrote a whole bunch of essays that are hard to understand." I try to think of what else. "Oh, and our school is named after him." I always do my homework, but I don't want to be one of those know-it-all kids who wave their hands around like they're trying to put out a fire whenever a teacher asks a question.

Ms. Jacobs writes my three things on the board and then looks around the class. No one says anything, but there's a lot of feet shuffling and readjusting in seats. "Anyone else?"

When no one else raises their hand, I wish I hadn't said anything.

Ms. Jacobs raps the end of the marker on the white-board. "Wake up, people! This is your life you're living.

You can't sleep through it." Ms. Jacobs says stuff like this a lot. She frowns at us and then gives a little sigh. "Shayla is right. He lived in the eighteen hundreds and he did quite a bit of writing." She gives me a tiny smile. "It can be a bit dense. But I'm surprised you didn't learn he was a passionate abolitionist, Shayla."

I slump in my seat and start picking at a tiny blob of ink stuck on my desk. I hate when a teacher assumes that just because I'm Black, I'll know all about slavery and civil rights and stuff like that. I'm the only Black student in the class, so I know everyone's staring at me, trying to see if I have bat wings or hairy armpits. Like being Black is a whole different species.

Living in West Los Angeles means there aren't a whole lot of people who look like me. It was worse in elementary school. At least at Emerson, there are a lot more Black kids. There's a lot more of everything in junior high. But you wouldn't know it in my English class. I sink even lower in my seat.

Ms. Jacobs gives another little sigh and then asks us, "How are everyone's eyeball journals coming along?"

I look down and hope someone will volunteer to talk about how wonderful their journal is. My journal is

still a whole lot of blank pages and some random observations that don't seem all that interesting.

The front doors of the school are silver.

My sandwich was yummy.

Yolanda had TEN braids on each side today.

I need better underwear.

When no one answers her, Ms. Jacobs says, "If you
don't have anything to write about, watch the news.
There have been a lot of stories lately that are important. Race factoring into police activity is something you
should pay attention to."

It feels like Ms. Jacobs is just talking to me again,
and it makes my whole face get hot. Momma and Daddy
were talking last night about how a police officer is
going to go on trial because she shot a Black man when
he was walking to his car. The video of him getting shot
got played over and over online. I sure don't want to
observe that anymore.

"You know, Emerson had a strong belief in the power of the individual. He believed *all* people were important. No matter their race."

I don't think I can get any lower in my seat. If Ms. Jacobs was a television, I'd change the channel.

"It was a pretty radical belief for his time. That type of thinking wasn't popular or well respected by many people back then. Emerson had to be fairly brave to be an abolitionist."

I would like to abolish this conversation.

5
Lockers & Lunch

As soon as Ms. Jacobs releases us, I shove my way down the crowded hallway to my locker.

Lockers are one thing I love about junior high. It might sound funny to say I love a scratched-up piece of bright yellow, clanky metal, but I *do*. I love spinning the little dial, pretending I'm an international jewel thief. And once I get my stuff out, or put my stuff in, giving the door a big slam is so satisfying.

After I fish out my lunch, I slam the door closed. All up and down the hallway the sound of locker doors slamming rings out. I head outside and meet up with Julia by the water machines. They used to be soda machines when my sister went here, but the school district got on a big antisugar kick since then.

"Where do you think Isabella went?" I ask. With

best friends, you always know what they are up to, but until break today, Isabella didn't breathe one word about leaving early.

"Probably a doctor's appointment," Julia says. "Come on. Let's go eat!" She whips my arm, making me spin off the walkway, cracking us both up. Julia gives great roller whips.

We grab each other's arms and race-walk to the lunch area.

Outside the gym, a shiny solar overhang shields a bunch of steel-blue tables in tidy rows. It's where kids sit who brought lunch; if you buy, then you go sit in the cafeteria. Isabella, Julia, and I always bring, so we sit in the overhang area. I like eating outside. Cafeterias stink. Too many food smells blending together. Fish-stick burritos? Yuck!

It's weird for it to be just me and Julia at lunch, and it's even weirder when, instead of heading to our normal lunch table, Julia stops at a table with a bunch of girls she knows from her Asian basketball league and her church.

She had wanted to sit there on the first day of school, but I told her I wanted it to be just us—the United Nations. What I didn't say was that I felt awkward with

Isabella and me being the only girls there who weren't Asian, because it seemed like the wrong thing to say even if it was true. I just walked us over to an empty table, and that's where we've been sitting ever since.

I don't know why Julia thinks we should change where we sit today just because Isabella isn't here, but it makes my hands itch all over to keep standing there when the girls are already squeezing over to make room for Julia and me.

One of the girls at the table is Stacy Chin. Everybody knows Stacy. She's really popular. She has a loud laugh and an even louder voice. Stacy always wears a lot of glittery eye makeup, and her black hair is streaked with bright magenta highlights. With her spaghetti-strap top and low-cut short shorts, she is basically a walking violation of Emerson's dress code.

The dress code is printed right in the handbook they mail out over the summer. It's hard to wear spaghetti-strap tops with a bra, so I don't mind there being a rule against them, and no way would my parents let me wear short shorts—to school or anywhere. But making sure skirts go past your fingertips seems dumb, because there's nothing cute about skirts that long, and not being able to wear solid red or solid blue is a pain. It's supposed to be a gang-violence thing, but since blue is one of our school's colors, not being able to wear it doesn't make a whole lot of sense.

Obviously, Stacy isn't worried one bit about getting in trouble for what she's wearing.

And the girl can *talk*. Like the seagulls that fly around the lunch tables, trying to steal someone's sandwich. Stacy is all *squawk, squawk, squawk*.

"Bruuhh," she says to Julia. "Can you believe Mr. Milton got all loud at me in history? I was about to go off on him!" She laughs and grabs a bunch of Cheetos from the girl next to her and shoves them into her mouth. Then she makes gagging noises. "Gross, Lynn! Your Cheetos are stale!" Stacy throws a Cheeto at Lynn, and Lynn bats it back at her. "These teachers need to know what's up, know what I'm sayin'?"

Lynn rolls her eyes, and I try really hard not to roll mine. Julia gives me a look like she's trying to warn me not to say anything. At least now I know better than to say, *No, I don't know what you're saying.*

"So my moms said I already had blue Vans, but these were totally different," Stacy says, sticking her legs out to show off her shoes. "Like I had to have these kicks, right? I totally got Pops to get 'em. You know how pops are."

It's hard to keep up with Stacy. I wonder if she just opens her mouth and waits to see what random thing will fly out of it.

All of a sudden, a girl at the next table over shouts, "Command!" and we all turn to see who got caught.

Almost everyone at Emerson is playing this game called Command. The rules are, you have to keep something crossed all the time, like your fingers or legs. If someone catches you uncrossed, they can command you to do whatever they want, and if you don't do it, they pound you.

I am not playing. Who wants to play a game where you can be commanded to do anything? Just call that game Itchy Hands. It feels like I'm the only person in our whole school who doesn't want to play, and that's cool with me.

It's easy to tell who got caught, because a few tables over, a girl's face is getting redder and redder while her friend whispers in her ear. Daddy talks a lot about what he calls white privilege, but if you ask me, getting so red that everyone can tell when you're embarrassed is no kind of privilege. Her blush makes it look like someone scribbled over her face with a red marker.

Blush girl slowly walks over to a table full of boys and stands in front of one of them. "I . . . I think you're really cute," she says, in a trembly voice.

The whole table of boys starts cracking up, and blush girl runs back to her friends and buries her face in her hands.

"That's all kinds of wrong," I mutter.

"That's all kinds of *hilarious*, you mean," Stacy says, clapping her hands like it was a great show. "We should totally command someone to do something crazy." She nudges Julia's arm.

"It's not going to be me," Julia says. "I'll always have something crossed." She holds up her hands and all her fingers are crossed over each other. It looks like someone broke her fingers.

"I didn't say it was going to be you," Stacy says, raising her eyebrows. "But I'm going to get somebody."

I shrug. "Well, I'm not even playing."

"Oh, yeah?" Stacy asks like she's daring me to something, and I get a bad feeling. A bad itchy-hand feeling.

"You're so mean, Stace," Lynn says. "You need to quit." Her long black hair is so shiny and pretty, it's like she polished it with Windex. When she gives me a big smile, I smile right back like we're sharing a joke.

Stacy ignores us and starts talking about how boring her computer elective is, and then everyone starts talking about their electives and how fun or awful they are. Electives are probably the thing I was looking forward to the most about junior high. In elementary school, you don't get to pick a class just because you like it. You don't really get to pick anything in elementary school. Julia is in chorus and Isabella is in art. I'm pretty sure Julia's mom made her take chorus, but Isabella loves anything creative.

"What's your elective?" Lynn asks me.

"Shop," I say.

Julia grins at me and I know what's coming. "But you don't even *like* shopping," she says.

Ha ha. Stacy cracks up like that's the best joke ever. I thought it was funny too, the first time Julia said it.

My elective is actually called Industrial Arts, and of course it has nothing to do with shopping.

"At least you get to be around Tyler," Julia says.

That's not funny; that's mean. "Quit it, Julia," I say. Tyler is a boy in shop with me, and Julia knows how irritating I think he is.

"Ooo," Stacy says. "Who's this Tyler?"

"Nobody," I say, giving Julia a warning look.

Julia looks at me like, *Oops*. I know she's just trying to be funny, but I'm going to have to tell her later to save that for when it's just us.

A few of the girls start talking about their last basketball game and how tough practice is going to be tonight. Usually when people talk about sports, I don't have anything to say. But now I realize I actually do.

"I think I might join the track team," I offer.

"Really?" Julia sounds shocked. She knows I'm not very coordinated, but come on. I can run, at least.

"Yes" is all I say.

Not only am I going to do track, I'm going to be awesome at it.

After lunch, Julia and I walk together to our next classes.

She turns to me and touches my arm. "Hey, it's cool you're going to be all athletic now. Maybe next you'll start playing basketball!" Then she cracks up.

"Yeah, I'll sign right up to play on the Tigers," I joke.

When Julia first told me you had to be Asian to play in her basketball league, it hurt my feelings. It seemed like the people who made the league were saying they didn't want me to play with them. But Daddy told me it wasn't about keeping me out; it was about lifting up the kids who played in the league. He made me watch some basketball games with him and count all the Asian players. The day we watched, I didn't see one, so I got it after that. Isabella and I have gone to watch Julia's team play a few times. Julia's really quick and makes a bunch of three-pointers. I think she's their best player.

"Is Tyler running track too?" Julia teases.

"You are so not funny. I can't stand him and you know it."

"I know. I'm sorry! I was just messing around," Julia says. "You know me." She grabs my arm and gives me a roller whip.

It's hard to stay mad when you're spinning around, and all I can do is laugh.

"Text me later!" Julia says, as we go our separate ways.

"I'll text you after I go *shopping*," I call after her, and smile. I can be funny too.

6

Tuna & Metal

I never knew metal had a smell, but it does. It's sharp and stings my nose as soon as I walk into sixth period.

I'm glad I have shop at the end of the day. After fifth period, my head is swimming with numbers and equations, and getting to make something pushes that all away.

I didn't really know what to expect when I signed up for shop. I've always liked making things, and when Daddy was a kid, he took wood shop and made a little bench we still use. I figured it would be fun. But I sure didn't think it would be almost all boys. On the first day, when I walked in and saw all those boys staring at me like I was a piece of hair in their soup, it sure felt good to see Yolanda's upside-down-Y smile. Since we're the only girls in the class, we cling together like staticky socks.

Shop is like taking a class at Home Depot. Instead of desks we have worktables and stools. One whole wall is lined with big power tools. I'm afraid of the table saw because there's a rumor a kid sawed the tips of his fingers off one year, but the rest of the equipment seems less scary. One machine can drill right through metal.

"Get your trays and get to work," Mr. Klosner says, his big fuzzy mustache waggling at us.

Yolanda and I grin at each other. We both think Mr. Klosner's mustache is hilarious. Especially the way when he's thinking about something, he'll twist the ends like he's trying to unscrew them.

I pull on the heavy work gloves Mr. Klosner likes us to wear. I feel ready to do serious business as soon as I put them on.

Even though Mr. Klosner said *trays*, my project doesn't look like much of anything yet. It's a small rectangle of metal, and I have to hit it over and over again with a riveting hammer until it is completely covered with little round divots. This will make the metal look more decorative—according to Mr. Klosner. Once I finish that step, I'll get to use a big machine with clamps so I can fold up the four edges of the metal rectangle.

And *then* I'll have a tray. I don't know what I'll do with it when it's done. Probably give it to Momma so she can put her bracelets on it or something.

Each time my hammer hits the metal, a tingling vibration flashes up my arm.

Tyler leans over, and I can smell the tuna he had for lunch. "So, yeah, uh, your tray looks really good." Tyler has tiny teeth and a huge smile.

"Thanks," I say, without making eye contact, and I shift away, hoping he can take a hint.

Tyler always gets too close whenever he talks to me, like he wants to share some great secret. I sure wish he'd stop.

I also wish he would breathe his tuna breath on someone else.

Tyler drums his fingers on our worktable. His nails are bitten to the quick. "You have, a, uh, pretty name and all."

Smoooooth.

Yolanda giggles and I want to kick her, but instead I just whack my project harder, making the metal bounce.

"I hear folks call you Shay sometimes. That's like me. Hardly nobody calls me Tyler. I go by Ty."

I keep pounding away. *Zing, zing,* up my arm.

Tyler puts his *very* sweaty hand on my arm. "Hey, girl, you don't have to kill the thing."

I jerk my arm away. "I'm not." I wish I could say what I'm thinking which is: *Bye, Ty.* "You're supposed to have your work gloves on."

He doesn't say anything to that, but he doesn't stop smiling at me either. Talk about annoying. Tomorrow I'm switching seats with Yolanda.

People with sweaty hands should keep them to themselves.

7
Sirens

Momma likes to pick me up after the long line of cars in the drop-off/pick-up zone has cleared out so she can just whisk to the curb. But I don't like sitting next to the flagpole by myself looking like I was forgotten.

Only a tiny group of kids is left by the time I finally see Momma's white SUV.

"Why are you so late?" I ask.

"Excuse me, did my child just ask me why I was taking time out of my busy day to come pick her up when she could catch a bus home?"

I know Momma isn't asking me a real question, and I decide to change the subject before I get into trouble. I tell her about Coach West asking me to come out for track and how I am going to do it. Momma starts laughing.

"Thanks," I say, and cross my arms tight. Momma

tells me and Hana all the time how she will always encourage us, but she's not going to lie to us either. She has never told me I am athletic like she tells Hana.

"Oh, I'm s-s-s-sorry," she says, seeing the look on my face. "But you? Running?" A whole fresh batch of laughter steams up the windows. She even has tears spouting.

"It's not funny," I say, but a small smile is trying to steal over my face. When Momma laughs like this, it's really hard not to laugh too, even when she's laughing at you. Her whole body gets into it. I try biting my lips from the inside, but before I know it, I'm laughing right along with her.

"I can't wait to come to one of your track meets," she says, getting herself together.

"No way," I say. My seat belt feels like it's pressing hard against my chest, and I have to pull it away from me. "You and Daddy can't come. I'd never be able to get down the track knowing you were busting a gut in the stands."

"Okay, baby, whatever you say," she says. "Now leave that seat belt alone."

I let it slap back and stare out the window. We pass a

house that looks like Hansel and Gretel might live there.

"How come you're not taking Wilshire?" I ask. Momma always takes the same route home, but today she's going a different way.

"There's some protesting going on. Causing a mess of traffic." Momma's fingers grip the steering wheel tighter.

"Protesting what?"

"That trial started today." Momma's voice is low and serious, and I wish we could go back to joking about track. "People are acting like they already know what the verdict's going to be."

"What do you think is going to happen?" I've heard my parents talking about what might happen if the police officer who shot that man isn't found guilty. They talk about it when they think I'm asleep.

"I don't know, sugar. I try to keep an open mind, but all these trials seem to end the same way. Doesn't seem like Black folks can get any justice."

"Is it Black Lives Matter doing the protest?"

"No," Momma says. "But people are squawking on the news anyway how it's Black Lives Matter causing the problem." She sighs and looks over her shoulder to change lanes.

I look behind me too and see a whole bunch of police cars. And then, just like me turning around flipped a switch or something, their lights start flashing and their sirens go on, and you bet I start thinking they're after us. "Pull over, Momma!"

"Don't worry, baby," Momma says, but her voice is tight. She pulls over and we watch the line of police cars whiz past us, their sirens shrieking.

After a second, Momma pulls back into traffic.

"Momma?" I chew on my lip for a minute, watching the blue and red lights get farther away. "Do the police hate us? Hate Black people?"

"Oh, no, honey, don't start thinking that." Momma gives my knee a little squeeze. "It's like . . ." She taps her nails on the steering wheel, thinking. "Okay, like if you eat unhealthy food a long time, you're going to be unhealthy, right? Well, for too long people have been fed a diet about Black folks. About folks with brown skin. Making them think we're scary. And that's how the police have been trained to act. It's going to take a long time to change people's minds."

"Maybe after the trial is over, people will know we're not scary. They'll know we matter."

"Oh, baby . . ." Momma shakes her head.

I reach over and pat her hand. "It'll be okay, Momma. There's a video this time. No way could anyone say that officer was innocent."

Momma doesn't say anything.

8
Pictures & Pits

When we get home, I go straight to my room without even stopping to get a snack like I normally do. I kick my shoes off and fall onto my bed.

My favorite thing in my room is my bulletin board, full of pictures of the United Nations—me, Julia, and Isabella in silly poses. Almost all of them are from those photo booths they have at malls and amusement parks. A line of four pictures that's almost always in black and white because that's the cheapest. I have loads of them. The pictures go all the way back to when we were little, and we're making goofy faces in most of them.

We'll probably take a ton of great ones this year. Too bad they don't have a photo booth at school.

Maybe someone will take a picture of me at a track meet. I imagine myself crossing the finish line first with everyone cheering and confetti shooting into the sky. That would be a great picture.

I flop over onto my belly and snuggle into my blankets. Momma must've just done laundry, because my sheets smell like Tide. I should start homework, but I'm too comfortable to move.

Then Hana walks in. My sister barges into my room whenever she feels like it, but if I go into her room without knocking, she cuts my head off.

"What's up?" she asks, as if *I* asked to talk to *her*. She takes a seat on my beanbag chair, and little bits of stuffing spill out from the seam.

Daddy says we look alike, but I'm still waiting for that to be true. We're both tall, but since Hana has always played basketball, for her it's a bonus. (Dad made me try and play basketball last year, but after getting an elbow in my eye, and me crying about it all over the court, we both decided the sport was not for me.)

We have the same hair (thick and sort of bushy) but she has hers figured out, while mine is usually a mess. She plucks her eyebrows into neat little arches, and her ears are pierced at the top, where it looks totally cool. She probably has a tattoo like most of her friends, but if she does, she keeps it hidden.

Hana always seems a little bit bored, as if there's something better going on and if you would just stop bugging her, she could get back to it. I hope by the time I'm a senior in high school, I will have mastered that look.

"I'm probably going to get killed in science," I say. I know I'm being a little dramatic, but it's nice having her attention. "I got partnered with Bernard. I told you about him. He's mean? Today he knocked his whole desk over."

"Why?"

"I think he didn't like getting yelled at."

"Mmm."

"It was scary, Hana!"

Hana sighs in that way that means she's just about done with me. "Bernard's that big kid, right?"

"Yes! He's huge!"

"And Black, right?"

"I don't think he's scary because he's Black, Hana. I think he's scary because he acts mean all the time."

Hana taps the black armband she's wearing and smirks at me. Hana and all her friends wear black armbands to show their support for the Black people who've died when dealing with the police.

"It's not about that," I argue.

Hana shrugs, and then her phone buzzes and she pulls it out. I can tell by the smile on her face that it's her friend Regina texting her. Hana gets all silly when she and Regina are together, or texting each other, or pretty much if you just say Regina's name.

Seeing that goofy smile on Hana's face is pretty funny. She looks completely un-Hana-ish.

"How's Regina?" I ask.

Hana's smile gets wide, but then she looks at me like I caught her rifling through Momma's purse, and she frowns at me. Yeah, that's the Hana face I know.

She shakes her head like I'm so exasperating. "Are you still sitting in the lunch pit? Or have you gone over by the basketball courts yet?"

When I first started at Emerson, Hana told me the Black kids sit by the basketball courts. Hana is really weird about race stuff. Not only does she tease me about not having Black friends, she *only* has Black friends.

"I sit at the lunch tables." I'm not going to call where we sit a *pit*. And I'm sure not going to tell Hana what table I sat at today. It would take more explaining than I know how to do to tell her how I sat with an Asian

46

group, when she's so annoyed I don't sit with the Black group. The whole thing seems pretty weird to me. In elementary school, we sat by grade, next to whoever our friends were. "I sit with my *friends*, Hana."

Hana goes back to her phone and types something in quick. I'm certain she and Regina are talking about me. "Eventually folks are gonna say you think you're too good. You know that, right?"

"What? I'm supposed to just sit with people I don't know? Jules and Is are my best friends." I point at my bulletin board. "We're the United Nations. Why would anybody have a problem with that?"

"Because," she says, like that is a real answer. "Anyway, don't be surprised if you and your little group don't end up . . ." Hana puts her hands together, and then splits them apart.

"You don't know what you're talking about, Hana." I'm almost yelling, and trust me, you don't want to yell at my sister.

"Okay, fine, Miss Thang," Hana says, getting up. "Don't say I didn't warn you. And be nice to Bernard." She walks out of my room and leaves my door wide open.

I get up and stop myself from slamming it, and just shut it quietly. Hana acts like she knows so much more than me about everything.

I grab the spiral notebook off of my desk. It seems like I finally have interesting stuff to write in my observation journal.

I can't believe Hana wants me to be nice to a bully.

I do not sit in a *pit*, and Hana is wrong about me and my friends. We are the UNITED NATIONS. Even with that trial going on, I still think Hana makes way too big of a deal over race. Isabella, Julia, and I know that for us, race doesn't even *matter*.

And what matters is us; Hana is being ridiculous if she thinks that me and my friends are going to split up.

9
Eyeballs

When we sit down for dinner that night, I wait until Daddy has a mouthful of steak before I ask my question. "Did I tell you guys I'm supposed to be an eyeball?"

Just like I thought, his cheeks go extra puffy because he's trying not to laugh and swallow at the same time.

"What, now?" Momma says.

"Like Ralph Waldo Emerson? Ms. Jacobs says he was really into observing, so that's what I've been doing. Observing. Like I'm an eyeball. And writing what I observe in my eyeball journal."

Daddy smirks at Momma. (He's a big smirker.) "They're teaching the dead white men a lot earlier these days, huh?" he says.

"Don't start, Richard," Momma says, but her voice is smiling.

"What? What do you mean?" I ask.

Before Daddy can answer, Momma cuts him off. "There's nothing wrong with learning about Emerson." She throws a look at Daddy. No one can toss a look like Momma. "Your father just means a lot—"

"Most," Daddy interjects.

"A *lot*," Momma repeats, "of the things you'll be taught at school are from . . . a certain perspective."

"Dead white men's perspective?" I ask.

"Bingo!" Hana says, grinning like she won something.

"But my school is *named* after him. That's why Ms. Jacobs said we should learn about him," I try to explain. "And he was an abolitionist!"

"Mm-hmm," Daddy says.

"Richard," Momma warns. "Shayla, it's great you're learning about Emerson. Especially at your age. I don't think I'd even heard of him until I met your father, who used to *quote* him all the time."

My eyes fly to Daddy. He has his bad-puppy-dog look going strong.

"'Make the most of yourself, for that is all there is of you,'" Daddy says. "That's one of my favorites." He sees the way I'm looking at him. "Hey, I never said I didn't like what the cat had to say. But they sure do need to expand what you all are exposed to. There's a whole lot of great thinkers who are people of color."

"I *know*, Daddy," I say. Sometimes my family acts like I don't know a thing about being Black.

"'Not everything that is faced can be changed,'" Daddy says, and then Hana cuts in and says, "'But nothing can be changed until it is faced.'"

"Is that an Emerson quote too?" I ask, and Hana elbows me hard in the arm. "Ow, quit, Hana!"

"That's James Baldwin," Daddy says.

"A *Black* man," Hana says.

I stare down at my plate, embarrassed I didn't know that.

10
Caterpillars

The next day in science, Mr. Levy gives us some free time at the end of class, and after rubbing my hands together really hard, I make my way up to his desk. I'm trying to force myself to ask him if I can switch partners, but Bernard is staring at me like he knows just what I'm going to say.

Mr. Levy's eyes are huge behind his glasses. "Yes?" he says to me.

"Are butterflies arthropods?" I ask. It was the first question to pop out, and I feel dumb because I know the answer.

"Yes, they are. We'll be looking at some lovely examples in our next lab."

Bernard starts walking to Mr. Levy's desk, and I panic. Thankfully, the bell rings, so I start to rush out of the class, but my backpack is on the floor, and I trip right over it.

Bernard breaks out into loud cackles.

It doesn't surprise me one bit that Bernard would laugh at me for falling down. I try not to look at him because I don't want him to see how mad I am.

In elementary school, Bernard would just step right in front of the first person in line for the rings like he was a big deal—which I guess he was—and no one would say a word. When he got ahold of the rings, he'd swing and laugh and kick his big Adidas at us until it was time to go back to class. Then he'd jump off and send the rings crashing into the middle pole with a clang that made me flinch.

Bernard grabs my hand and yanks me up, and I sprawl right into him like I'm one of those rings clanging into the pole.

I push away and grab my backpack from the floor.

"You don't got to break her, bruh," someone says, and from the tingly feeling I get in my stomach, I know exactly who that someone is.

I look straight into eyes so deep green, you'd think they were apple Jolly Ranchers.

Jace chuckles and slaps Bernard on the back, and then he walks out before I have time to say I'm not broken. Or maybe I am just a little bit, because I can't seem to make my mouth work right.

"I hurt you?" Bernard says, his mouth twisted into a knot.

I clear the butterflies out of my throat. "Nah, I'm good."

"Get to class," Mr. Levy says.

"That's what we're doing," Bernard says, and he brushes past me hard enough to almost make me fall down again.

But I don't care. All I can think is *Jace smiled at me.*

In second period, when Mr. Powell hands back a history test and I see I only got a 92 when this boy in my class, Alex, got a 94, I don't even care. Usually, Alex and I compete to see who can get the highest grade, and when I lose, it really bothers me, but not today. *Jace smiled at me.*

Still, I still can't help saying to Alex, "Don't get too comfortable. You just got lucky this time."

"Oh, you got jokes?" Alex says. "We'll see, smart

girl." He gives me this serious nod that cracks me up.

At break, I plop down under our magnolia tree, next to Isabella and Julia. I'm just about to tell them about Jace when I stop and look at Isabella. "You look different," I say, squinting at her, trying to figure it out.

"You got your braces off!" Julia exclaims, and I see she's right.

Isabella hadn't said one thing about getting her braces off when we were all texting last night. And the only pictures she posted online were of Kahlo, one of her cats, and her swollen toe after she stubbed it.

"I can't believe you didn't tell us," Julia says accusingly.

I mean, seriously. We tell each other everything. "*Why* didn't you tell us?" I ask. And then I notice something else. "You got your eyebrows done too?" I don't think my voice could get any more high-pitched. I have caterpillars for eyebrows, and I try to talk Momma into letting me get them waxed, but she says N-O. (She really does spell it out, as if that makes it sound more case-closed. Which, actually, it does.)

"I wanted to surprise you," Isabella says. Then she blushes and drops her head, letting her hair fall into her face. "My mom wanted me to lose the unibrow more than I did." She glances up at us and then back down. "I don't look weird?"

"You look *scorching*," Julia says. And she doesn't sound jealous at all.

Isabella bumps her with her shoulder.

"Jace smiled at me," I say, needing to change the subject.

"Oh, well, I guess he's going to be your boyfriend tomorrow, then," Julia says, and giggles.

"Why do you want a boyfriend anyway?" Isabella asks.

I wish I had a good answer for this. Last year in sixth grade I liked this boy Joshua, but he asked Brianna Merkins to be his girlfriend. Brianna has long blond hair she's always swinging around. And when people would tell her that her and Joshua made a cute couple, she would get this look. This *I know* look. I want to be able to give that look. I don't want to say that, though. "Because we're in seventh grade now," I say instead.

Julia says, "Jace *is* super *fine*." Then she says, "He'll probably end up with someone gorgeous."

And then . . . she glances over at Isabella.

I look at Isabella too. With her nonbushy hair, big hazel eyes, regular-sized forehead, perfectly groomed eyebrows, and shiny straight teeth.

I do not like what I see.

Even though the bell hasn't rung, I say, "Break's over," and get up for class.

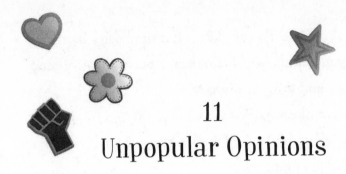

11
Unpopular Opinions

For the first time I wish we had to run the mile in PE. I need a good run to get rid of all the thoughts banging around in my head. I know it's not right for me to be jealous of Isabella, but I can't help it.

Coach West does have us do some sprints, and that helps a little even though I'm not one of the fastest kids. Not by a long shot.

Carmetta is faster than everybody. I've never seen anyone move that fast in real life. It makes me think twice about joining the track team. What if everybody else can run fast like Carmetta?

But toward the end of class, when Coach West tells everyone who's joining track to huddle up, I huddle.

"We'll have our first practice next Tuesday, okay? Make sure you tell your parents, guardians, grandparents, or whoever will be wondering where you are after school. If you don't have running clothes, your PE clothes will be fine."

My ugly PE clothes will *not* be fine. I wonder if Momma will buy me running clothes. I sigh. Momma's not a big fan of buying me stuff she's not a hundred percent sure I need.

Yolanda and I rush to the locker room together.

"You should ask Coach West if you can be on the track team too," I say.

"Have you seen me run?" Yolanda laughs. Today her hair is in two buns, one on either side of her head.

"Will you at least change seats with me in shop?" I ask her. If she isn't willing to do track, maybe she'll at least do this one favor.

She shrugs. "Sure," she says. "I don't care where I sit."

Then we split up for our different rows. Once I'm changed back into my regular clothes, I can't wait for her. I have to run all the way across campus to get to English.

When I get to class, I settle into my seat, breathing hard like I just finished a race.

Ms. Jacobs gives me a look like my heavy breathing is bothering her, and then she asks if anyone wants to share anything from their eyeball journals. No one does. I know I sure don't.

"Nobody?" she asks, sounding disappointed. "Afraid of what your friends might think?" She writes a quote on the board:

"Do not go where the path may lead, go instead where there is no path and leave a trail."
—*Ralph Waldo Emerson*

"What does that mean to you?" Ms. Jacobs asks the class.

I picture myself alone in the woods, lost and crying. You bet I don't say that.

A skinny girl raises her hand. "To make up your own mind?"

Someone else says, "Be a leader instead of a follower?"

Ms. Jacobs nods. "It's hard, but you can't always worry about what everyone else thinks. It's important to decide what *you* believe in and stick with it. Emerson thought that was important, and he wasn't afraid to have unpopular opinions. I believe, if he were alive now, he would be a strong supporter of the Black Lives Matter movement."

I believe, if Emerson were alive now, Ms. Jacobs would want to marry him, the way she talks about him all the time.

"Emerson was *Black*?" Jay Landis shouts, and Ms. Jacobs narrows her eyes at him.

"No, Jay, he was not."

"Then why would he say only *Black* lives mattered?"

"What do you think, Shayla?" Ms. Jacobs asks me.

"I—I don't know." I squirm in my seat. Ms. Jacobs should really stop acting like just because I'm Black, I'm the only one in class who has an opinion about Black stuff. I don't know how to answer her. I mean, I know Black Lives Matter is about reminding people our lives count too, but some people take it wrong and think it means we are saying our lives matter *more* than theirs. Or that *only* our lives matter. But Momma explained it to me. She said if you go to the doctor and told him you broke your arm and he said, *Well, okay, let's put you in a full-body cast,* you'd say, *But, doctor, only my arm is broken.*

Get it? So yeah, even though all your bones matter, you only need to fix the broken one. (Momma said it a lot better.)

A boy in the back calls out, "My dad says saying Black lives matter is racist."

I want to tell him his dad is an idiot, but I pinch my lips together and don't say anything. The back of my neck gets so hot, I think I might burn right up.

Ms. Jacobs rests a hand on my shoulder. I'm not sure if she guesses there's a whole pot of bubbling anger inside of me and she's holding me down before I start something, or if she is telling me everything's okay.

"Martin, if I tell you *your* life matters, do you think I'm saying nobody *else's* life in this class matters?" Ms. Jacobs's voice is calm and quiet.

Martin shakes his head, but I can tell he still doesn't get it. I wonder if I should tell him Momma's bone story.

"So when African Americans say Black lives matter, can you see how they aren't saying that other people's lives don't matter?"

It takes Martin a minute, but he finally nods. I don't care. I still think his dad is a dummy.

Someone in the back of the class—it sounds like

Amy Teen—says, "But why are the protests so angry?"

"You'd be angry too if people who looked like you were getting shot for no reason," I say, sort of under my breath and sort of not, and then snap my mouth back closed. I don't know how those words sneaked out. It's like my mouth has a mind of its own. I hear some whispering behind me but I don't look.

Ms. Jacobs gives my shoulder a squeeze, but then she releases it. "Injustice usually makes people angry," she says. "Some people are confused about why businesses get vandalized in protests. That can seem wrong. But I'm not sure what is the right way to act if people in your community seem to be unfairly targeted by the police."

Momma and Daddy don't want me watching the videos of Black people getting shot or choked or beat up by police. But there's been so many of them, I can't help but see some. And I've seen videos of protests too, and sometimes they do get really loud and scary.

Ms. Jacobs says, "I can't tell you what to think. I know in class and at home, and with your friends, you will hear lots of different things. And some of those things will be right and some will be wrong. You're going to have to use those brains of yours to figure out the difference. Really pay attention to what you're seeing and make up your own mind."

I wish she would just tell Martin-with-the-dumb-dad that his father is wrong.

Ms. Jacobs hits her marker against her hand and stares at us for a second. Then she turns to the board and writes:

"No one is born hating another person because of the color of his skin, or his background, or his religion. People must learn to hate, and if they can learn to hate, they can be taught to love. . . ."

It takes her a while to write all those words, and no one makes a peep while she's writing.

"Does anyone know who said that?" she asks us.

"Barack Obama!" someone shouts out.

"Well, he did tweet it. But he was quoting someone else." Ms. Jacobs turns around and writes *Nelson Mandela* underneath the quote. "Mandela was a brave man and a powerful leader. And he made me believe that it's possible for things to change." Ms. Jacobs smiles, but I feel like her words are just for me.

I can't wait to tell Daddy that Ms. Jacobs taught us something that wasn't from a dead white man's perspective. But I wish she'd stop acting like I'm the only one in class who would understand a *Black* perspective. If I can understand a dead white man, then everyone else should be able to understand what someone Black has to say.

I also don't get why some people would think Black people are against *them* when *we're* the ones getting shot.

12
Super Salty

At lunch, Isabella, Julia, and I sit in our regular lunch spot, even though I notice Julia looking over at the table we sat at yesterday.

I bet she wants to sit there, but that's not our spot. Lynn seems nice, but I'm not sure about Stacy, and besides, the United Nations sit together, just the three of us.

"So tell us more about Jace smiling at you!" Isabella says. She has a little red speck on her cheek, probably paint from art class.

"Yeah, tell us all about it, bruh," Julia says, as if she already knows my story won't be all that exciting.

"Well, first, I fell down and Bernard almost gave himself a heart attack laughing at me."

"That's so not cool," Julia says, shaking her head.

"I know," I say. "And then he yanked me up *super* hard." I'm putting a little extra sauce on my story, but that's what makes a story good. "Jace wanted to make sure Bernard hadn't hurt me. Isn't that sweet? And then he smiled real big at me." Talking about it makes the butterflies come back.

"Sounds promising," Julia says, and I totally forgive her for sounding so sarcastic a minute ago.

"Command!"

I flinch when I hear the shout.

A bunch of boys surround Alex, and I can tell they're being jerks just by how they're laughing and nudging each other.

One of the boys, Daniel Richards, says something to Alex, and at first Alex looks around, a little confused. Daniel is obnoxious, so I know whatever he said can't be good.

"Why can't they leave him alone?" I ask.

"Maybe he shouldn't crack on people all the time," Julia says. "Or be so sarcastic."

"You're one to talk," I tell Julia.

"They're just having fun," Isabella says. "It's not like they're hurting him. It's just a game." She sounds like she's apologizing even though she's not the one doing anything wrong.

Alex climbs up on a lunch bench. The big grin he usually wears is gone and he seems nervous.

"He doesn't look like he's having fun," I say.

Alex almost falls when he steps up from the bench to the top of the table, and instead of helping him, the boys just laugh harder. I start to get up, and that's when I see Jace standing right in the middle of it all, laughing with the rest of them. My throat gets really small and I sit back down. I'm not sure what I was going to do anyway.

I look around for Principal Trask. She likes to walk around at lunch making sure we're all doing what we're supposed to. This isn't what we're supposed to do. I know that for sure. Principal Trask is pretty scary, and if she has ever smiled, no one has told me about it. Normally, I don't want to see her, but I wish she'd show up and tell those boys to leave Alex alone.

"Sing it!" Jace shouts.

"Yeah, sing!" another boy calls out.

Alex starts singing that commercial jingle about good-smelling shampoo, but in the commercial it's a girl singing it, and I know the boys are trying to make

Alex feel embarrassed. Daniel is elbowing his friends and cracking up.

But then I see Alex's expression change, and his grin comes back. He starts clapping his hands, changing the beat, and I have no clue what he's up to.

Then he starts rapping! He lays down a few lines about how all the boys are jealous of his hair and need to try his shampoo. When he tells Daniel to stop whining, lots of people at the lunch tables start laughing, and you bet that makes Daniel get a big frown on his face. Serves him right. Alex fluffs his curly hair and then throws in a little beat box. When he's done, he takes a deep bow.

People start clapping and laughing. I bet they're all glad to see the tables get turned on Daniel too.

Daniel says, "Dude, that was wack," and gives Alex a mean look.

Then a yard-duty teacher comes over, and Daniel and Jace and the other boys run off, leaving Alex standing up on the table. The yard-duty teacher offers her hand to help Alex down, but he waves her off.

"I got it," he says.

"We don't climb on tables," she says.

I want to tell the teacher that she should be mad at

the boys who made Alex get on the table, but I don't want to get Jace in trouble.

"My apologies," Alex says, back to his goofball self, before dashing off.

I would've died if someone had made me get up on a table and sing. "I can't believe you two are playing that dumb game," I tell Isabella and Julia.

"Oh, come on," Isabella says. "If me and Julia are playing, you have to play." She has her ring finger crossed over her pinkie.

"No, she doesn't," Julia says. "We don't have to do everything together."

I hold my fist out for Julia to bump. "Yeah. I believe in the power of the individual."

"I'm never going to get caught, because I'll *always* have something crossed," Isabella says. She crosses her eyes at me, cracking herself up. Even with her eyes crossed, and paint on her face, Isabella looks pretty.

Julia hands Isabella a napkin. "You have a paint smudge," she says. "With all your new gorg, we can't have you going around with a smudgy face."

I squeeze my hands tight together to keep from saying anything. I don't know why Julia keeps making such a big deal about how pretty Isabella is.

Then Julia tells Isabella, "I bet you'll be the first of us to get a boyfriend, Is."

"Well, I *am* in love," Isabella says, and my stomach squeezes tight.

"What? Who with?" I demand.

Isabella looks all around before sliding out her phone. Having your phone out at school is big-time against the rules. As soon as she shows us the picture, Julia snorts.

"A *cat*?" Julia says. "Don't even mess around with us like that."

Isabella quickly shoves her phone back into her pocket. "Not a cat, a kitten. And isn't he the cutest? Just a sweet pile of fluff. He's like a tiny cloud."

"He is adorable," I say, feeling oddly relieved, "but your mom is never going to let you get another cat. You already have *three*." Isabella *loves* cats.

"My dad has a new girlfriend," Isabella says. "And you know my mom. She's all freaked out about it, and worried that *I'm* going to freak out about it, so she might say yes to a kitten."

When Isabella's parents first got divorced, they both bought her a lot of stuff as if they were competing to see which one she'd pick to love best. That seemed just plain silly to me. It's not as if she was divorcing *them*.

"And if she says no, I'll ask my dad," Isabella says. "He needs a pet."

"Okaaay," Julia says. "But I was talking about boys."

"My mom says boys are nothing but trouble," Isabella says.

I have to laugh. "My mom says the same thing."

"Just wait," Julia says. "I bet I'm right. You'll be the first to have a boyfriend, bruh."

"Save me from that drama," Isabella says, rolling her eyes.

Save me too. "She's not a bruh," I tell Julia.

Julia blows hair out of her face with a huff. "Don't be so salty, Shay."

I'm a big bag of barbecue chips salty.

13
Facials

I know Daddy loves me as much as Hana, but some-times he looks at my long legs and long arms like they're such a waste. After basketball was a total fail for me, he thought volleyball could be good. He got really excited thinking I could be the volleyball version of Serena Williams. But I was terrified of getting a "facial." That's when the ball smacks you right in the face. I saw it happen once. The girl's face was so red, and not just because she was crying really hard. Volleyballs are harder than dodgeballs!

But there are no balls in track. And really no elbows either. That's part of the reason I decided even I can run around a track without getting into too much trouble, or at least not get an elbow in my eye.

But after having a whole week to think about it, I'm

sure I'm making a mistake. I just don't know how to get out of it. So, on the first day of track practice, I walk real slow to the locker room, dreading changing, dreading running, dreading doing this at all without a friend.

I'm especially not happy about having to wear my PE clothes. I know how bad I look in the horrible shorts and bright yellow T-shirt. I should've asked Momma to take me shopping over the weekend, but I was afraid I was going to chicken out about going to practice.

The locker room is empty when I get there; everyone else must've already changed. I send Isabella and Julia a group text.

Me: Am I crazy for doing track?
Isabella: I think you're brave!
Julia: 😂 😂 😂

Nice.

I shuffle outside. This is the first time I hope Jace is not around. If he sees me in my PE clothes, I will never have a chance with him.

A bunch of kids stand around waiting, and my palms get all itchy because there is a small group of Black kids standing together. Carmetta is one of them. I don't know if I should go over there. That might sound like I don't know I'm Black, which isn't true. But I don't know how to walk over and act like I belong.

Sweat forms on my big forehead, and I rub my hands on my ugly PE shorts.

"Shay!" someone hollers.

I bite back a tiny scream. Bernard. Standing next to him is like standing next to a mountain.

"Uh, you run track?" I squeak. Nothing about Bernard makes me think he can run fast. Which is maybe a good thing. I could totally get away if he starts chasing me.

"Shot put," he says.

"Uh . . . ?" I don't like the sound of anything that has the word *shot* in it.

"It's a heavy thing you have to throw," Bernard says, like I should have known that. He puts up a hand to shield the sun out of his eyes and licks sweat off his upper lip.

Coach West comes outside and herds us all together.

"Okay, everyone, we're going to stretch it out, and then once we've got those muscles ready to go, we'll do a quick warm-up. Then we'll do a few drills so you can all get an idea of what's involved. Carmetta? Show everyone the stretches we want them to do, and then release them for four times around the track." Coach West sounds excited, like she's ready to find the next US Olympic track star.

A mile is our *warm*-up? Uh-oh.

Carmetta shows all the newbies like me the proper way to stretch. And then, too soon, it's time to run a mile.

"You like running?" Bernard huffs as we start our first lap.

I don't know why he is running with me except maybe because I'm slow and he is slow. "I guess?" I huff back. I start running faster, and now it feels exactly like Bernard is chasing me.

After our mile warm-up, Coach West explains how we're going to try a bunch of different things, and she assigns us to groups. I'm relieved I'm in a different one than Bernard.

I jump a few hurdles, run a 50 and a 100—I don't think I'm much of a sprinter—try to high-jump, and foul out a bunch of times on the long jump. Coach West has some of the eighth graders taking notes and keeping track of our times. Angie Watkins is one of the helpers.

Angie has long eyelashes that she makes even longer with mascara. She has on cute spandex track shorts, and although she isn't very tall, she has long, strong legs. Her hair is braided in a complicated pattern that she must've sat for hours to get. We are both Black, but we don't look anything alike. Although if I was allowed to wear mascara, I could at least have long eyelashes like hers, and that would be *something*.

When she sees me try to jump over some hurdles, she smiles at me. I smile back, but it makes me trip over the hurdle, and I almost fall right on my face. Angie puts her hand over her mouth quick, I guess to hold back all her laughter. I can't exactly blame her. I don't know what it is about someone falling that seems so funny.

After Coach West says we're done for the day, I head to the line at the water fountain to get a drink. Someone behind me bumps that space right at the back of my knee.

"Hey!" I say, whipping around.

Bernard.

My throat gets tight. "Sorry," I mumble, even though he nudged me.

"Got you," he says, pointing to my leg and laughing.

I turn back around. I don't want to be pounded.

"You did good," he says to my back.

It takes me a second to realize he paid me a compliment. "Thanks," I say, confused. I take my turn at the water fountain, wondering why he would be nice all of a sudden. When I finish slurping, I turn around and Bernard is still standing there like I'm supposed to say something else. "I, uh, like the hurdles," I say. I wipe water off my mouth. "But they're hard. I guess you need really good timing." I overheard Angie tell that to Carmetta.

"It's rhythm!" he shouts. "Can't you dance?" He starts dancing around me, which of course makes a bunch of kids look over.

I freeze. My face is so hot, it feels like someone smacked it with a ball.

Angie comes over and says, "Oh, that's what I'm talking about." And she starts dancing too. She swings her head around, making her braids swirl. Then she gives Bernard a little push and walks off.

Bernard laughs and then he gives *me* a little push. Except a push from Bernard is like a really hard shove, and I stumble back into the water fountain.

It doesn't exactly hurt, but it sure doesn't feel great.

Coach West signals me to come over. I just know she's going to say she made a big mistake and I don't need to come back to practice.

"Looks like you could use some better-fitting shorts," she says.

I nod happily. It feels like the first good thing that's happened in forever.

Doesn't it just figure that if Bernard is doing track, he'd do something that sounds like there is a gun involved?

I wish I looked like Angie Watkins. I wish I was Angie Watkins.

For the record, I actually CAN dance.

14
Broken

When Momma picks me up after practice, I tell her it was fine. "I think we're supposed to have running clothes, though."

"Mm," she says. She looks at me out of the corner of her eye, and for a second she has her N-O face going, but then she says, "Maybe we can go to Big 5 this weekend."

At home I write in my eyeball journal about Isabella being so cute now, and Bernard chasing me at track practice, and how bad I felt for not standing up for Alex. He's my friend, and I didn't say anything because I didn't want to make Jace mad. I know what a friendship manual would say about that.

But maybe Jace was just going along because he didn't know how to stand up and do the right thing. I bet he felt bad about it after.

On my phone, I have a video from the first week of school when we had a Spirit Day and Jace and some of his friends did some coordinated dance moves. It wasn't that impressive, but I was glad I had an excuse to video him.

He's so cute.

If he was my boyfriend, I'd tell him to be nice to people.

I think about that a whole bunch until Momma calls me for dinner.

Momma made chili for dinner, and it's just the way I like it, super spicy with hardly any beans. I notice Momma and Daddy don't talk about that trial at all while we eat. I think they don't want to worry me, and they probably don't want to get Hana started. She gets so mad about the police shootings, it's almost like she knew the people who got shot. Like they were her best friends or something. I'm bothered about it too, but I guess it makes me more scared than angry.

I decide to ask Momma a question that's bugged me about her broken-bone story. "Momma, when you were telling me about Black Lives Matter being like a bone, were you saying that Black people are broken?"

Momma passes me the water jug because she can tell my face is getting all steamed up from the heat of the chili. "No, sugar, we're not broken. We're just the ones who need attention right now."

"Because people keep trying to break us," Hana says. She claps after each word.

Momma cuts her eyes at Hana. "You keep focusing only on the bad in this world, and that's all you'll ever have."

"It's not *my* fault so many brothers are getting killed," Hana says.

Sometimes Hana gets really close to the line of talking back. As I'm pouring myself some water, making sure I get some ice, I take a quick peek at Momma to see if this is one of those times when Hana crossed the line, but Momma just looks sad instead of angry.

"I'm going to Regina's," Hana says, and starts to get up from the table.

I frown at my bowl. I'm not finished yet, but I'm close, which is supposed to mean we're at the part of dinner I like best, when the four of us are sitting at the dining table, knowing it's time to get up and put our plates in the dishwasher, but being too full to move. Daddy will usually crack jokes, and Momma sometimes will tell stories about back when she was a kid. Momma is the youngest of ten kids, and her brothers and sisters were always terrorizing her. She probably didn't think it was funny then, but she makes it seem funny now.

"Excuse you?" Momma asks Hana, not really asking anything. "Did I hear a question just now?"

Hana sets her bowl back down and twists her hands up like she's praying hard. "Can I pleeeeease go over to Regina's?"

"It's a school night," Momma says.

"But we need to make Black Lives Matter posters." Hana's eyes are all shiny, and I can't tell if she's excited about making posters or if it's just her usual reaction to seeing Regina.

I see Momma and Daddy exchange a look, and I know they will let Hana go. They are serious about school nights, but they are more serious about Black Lives Matter.

Momma tells Hana, "You better hurry and get going, Miss Thing, so you won't be out too late."

I wonder if Ms. Jacobs is right. Would Emerson really support Black Lives Matter even though he's a (dead) white man?

15
Sisters & Brothers

It's late and I'm in bed, but I am not having much luck getting to sleep.

When I think too much about Jace, I feel happy and sad at the same time. Maybe he will never like me back. And I want to have a thing. Julia has basketball and a whole group of other friends, and Isabella has art and is all beautiful now, so she has that too. Hana has Regina and Black Lives Matter. All I have is an eyeball journal. If Jace liked me back, I'd have a really good thing.

When I hear the front door open and close, I know Hana is home.

I hear her murmuring with Momma and Daddy and then I hear her in her bedroom. A few minutes later, I hear the bathroom door, and I risk creeping out of bed.

I bet Hana can tell me how to get Jace to notice me.

I knock softly on the bathroom door, and with a huff, Hana says, "Come in."

She's wrapping her hair up for the night, and I go ahead and risk joining her in the bathroom. Hana likes me to leave her alone mostly, and interrupting her nighttime routine makes my hands itch, but I have to ignore them.

Hana doesn't even look at me for a few minutes; then finally she says, "What?"

"I have a question about . . . um . . . boys." I start fiddling with the cream hand towels that are just for decoration. The towel we use for actual hand drying is on the counter.

"You don't need to be dealing with no boys," she says, but then maybe because she knows she sounded way too much like Momma, she sets her comb down and faces me. "Somebody trying to talk to you?" She sounds so serious, I worry that this was a bad idea.

"No," I say. Obviously boys talk to me, but that's not what Hana means. *Talking* means liking each other. Before you are boyfriend-girlfriend, you are *talking*. So far I haven't been talking with anyone.

Hana's eyes narrow like she's trying to see me better. "Then what?"

I'm not used to having my sister's attention focused all on me, and I start talking too fast. "There's a guy in my first period who's really cute. He has the greenest eyes and he makes everyone laugh all the time." Thinking about Jace gets me all tingly, like small moths are settling all over my arms and legs. It's a strange feeling. I don't even know if I like it.

"Is he nice?" Hana asks.

I ignore that question, because that's not really the point. "Julia said that Isabella will probably get a boyfriend before either of us do." I still can't believe she said that. Like Isabella is all that, and I'm just a five-head pile of dog food.

"Not everybody wants a boyfriend, you know," Hana says.

"But Jace is really cute. I'll show you." I search through my phone and pull up the video of Jace.

Hana stares at my phone for a minute. "He's a *brother*?" she asks, all shocky voice.

"So?" I say.

Hana hands me back my phone. "I'm surprised he's

Black. I didn't know you would be down with that."

"Ha, ha," I say, and it's all I can do not to roll my eyes at her.

"Check out little sis," Hana says, like she's showing me off to someone. "Next thing you know, you'll be protesting with me. You want me to get you an armband?"

Hana told me she wears her armband to make sure people don't forget about us mattering. To remember those who died. The armbands might make people remember, but it also seems like it might make people angry, and that's sure to be trouble, so I tell Hana, "No thanks."

Hana grips my arm hard. "Black Lives Matter is important, Shayla."

"I know!" Hana thinks I don't care about being Black sometimes since I'm not like her, but she's wrong. "I want people to know we matter too. I just don't want to wear an armband." If I started wearing an armband, everyone would ask me about it and make a big deal. And I don't think it would stop anyone from *dying*.

Hana sighs really loud, like she is in pain or something. "You can't just want things. Sometimes you have to *do* something. Like if you want that boy to notice you, you can't just sit there waiting for it to happen." Then she tells me to get out of the bathroom.

I'm back in my room before I realize she didn't tell me *what* I'm supposed to do to get Jace to notice me. No, not to notice me, but to *like* me.

Family is the most important thing ever, so when you think of Black people as a big family, it's easier to get why we say *Black lives matter.* I *know* Black Lives Matter is important—*obviously.* Hana acts like I'm dumb sometimes. But does she ever get embarrassed wearing her armband? Doesn't she worry people will think she's trying to start some trouble?

Until Hana said it, I didn't even think about Jace being a brother.

16
All the Girls

Momma busts me before I make it out of the house in the morning.

"Oh, no, ma'am!" Momma says, with one hand on her hip and the other clenching the car keys. "I *know* I do not see a bunch of junk on your face."

Hana told me I had to *do* something, and wearing makeup to school somehow seemed like a good idea, even though it's against Momma's rules. I don't know what I was thinking, though. It's not like I don't have to sit next to her on the way to school.

"But Momma, all the girls—"

"Did I hear you right? Are we *all the girls* all of a sudden? What have I told you about makeup?"

My head hangs even lower. "Not to wear it," I mumble.

"So why are you about to step outside looking like a clown?"

"I don't—" I cut myself off. There is no point arguing that I don't look like a clown even though I actually think I look good.

"If you don't go and wash your face this minute, you're gonna wish you had."

I pass Hana on my way to the bathroom, and she jabs me with an elbow.

"Dummy," she hisses at me. "Everybody knows you have to sneak the makeup to school and put it on there. Don't you know anything?"

No. I don't.

Once we get in the car, I'm sure Momma will keep on lecturing me, but instead she has the news radio on. They're talking about the trial.

"Why do they even need a trial?" I ask Momma. "Everyone saw the video."

"That's not how it works. Both sides get to make a case. Attorneys are telling the jury why they're right and the other side is wrong." Momma's face tightens some when she says the word *wrong*.

"But how can . . ." I don't know what to ask exactly.

It seems so obvious to me that the police officer acted wrong.

Maybe Momma could guess what I was struggling with, because she says, "The officer claims she feared for her life, so they'll talk about that." She reaches over and changes the station to the pop one she and I both like, but I know she doesn't feel like singing to Beyoncé right now.

"I don't get it. He was walking away from her. How could that be scary?"

"Shayla, stop fussing with me right now. You're giving me a headache."

I stay quiet for the rest of the drive.

17
History

Momma didn't want to talk about the trial, but Mr. Powell sure does.

"Our country has so many great things, but it also has a long history of intolerance. Sometimes trials like this one are . . . benchmarks. They can show how far we've come, or how far we've yet to go."

Alex raises his hand. "Why do people get upset just because someone's different from them?"

Mr. Powell wears bright-colored scarves, and whenever he's thinking hard on one of our questions, he'll play with the edge of the fabric, like he's searching the seam for an answer. "That's a great question, Alex," he finally says. "Sometimes people are scared about differences."

I think about Momma saying how the police officer

said she was afraid, and that makes me mad.

"That's not fair," I say.

"No, it isn't," Mr. Powell answers me. "Probably none of the reasons are fair. Ignorance. Fear. Anger. Jealousy." He ticks off the reasons on his fingers. "But you all are so young." He holds up his hands like a flood of arguments came storming at him. "I know you probably don't think so. You must think you're grown." He chuckles at that, and almost everybody in the class groans. "But you can be different from the generations before you. You can celebrate people's differences. Or step up and challenge beliefs you know are wrong. When this trial is over, whichever way the verdict goes, there's going to be a group of people who are angry."

I don't want to call Mr. Powell a liar, but what he said doesn't make sense to me at all. Right is right and wrong is wrong, and I don't see how people can be angry over that.

I raise my hand. "Mr. Powell, don't you think the jury is going to find the officer guilty?"

Mr. Powell rubs the edge of his scarf. "I don't know, Shayla. Sometimes all we can do is hope for change."

"What if it doesn't happen? Change, I mean?" I feel

a fluttering in my chest. It's like when you think something scary is about to happen in a movie.

"Then sometimes we have to fight for it," Mr. Powell says. Then he clears his throat and claps his hands. "Okay, let's get back to World War Two. We were looking at causes." He turns to the board and starts writing a bunch of dates.

I hate how much of history seems to be about fighting. With a sigh, I click my pen and start taking notes. I write down pretty much everything Mr. Powell says. Next test, I'm going to get the best grade in the class.

I check the big clock over the door. Class is almost over.

Sometimes Mr. Powell will let us out right before the bell for break, which is awesome. It means we can escape into the hallway before it fills up with people, all pushing and shoving, trying to get outside.

But today, when I'm anxious to get to my friends to tell them about my makeup fail, Mr. Powell takes forever to finish writing the history assignment on the board, and we can't leave class until after the bell.

I jam down the hall. Twelve minutes goes awfully fast.

Outside, I find Julia in a tight circle with the group of girls we sat with at lunch the other day, instead of waiting for me with Isabella like she's supposed to.

"Jules," I say, and try to grab her arm to pull her away.

Julia says, "Oh, hey." She moves her arm out of my reach and turns back to Stacy, who is talking like a tidal wave.

It's like Julia is obsessed with Stacy or something, and I'm trying hard not to feel annoyed.

"Check it, right?" Stacy says. "He was playin' all low key, but I know he was peeping me."

I don't know who Stacy is talking about. Whoever it was probably was just trying to figure out if that much glitter on her eyelids causes any permanent damage. I make another grab for Julia's arm, but she dodges it.

"Anyway, I had, like, *zero* chill. Inside, I was all, like, yaaas! You know what I'm sayin'?" Stacy nudges me. "Sister, *you* feel me, right?"

I don't know why Stacy is using the code for *We are Black girls*. Stacy is Chinese. "Come on, Jules," I say. "We need to find Is."

Julia gives me a weird look like I said something

wrong, then smiles at Stacy. "I feel you, Stace."

My hands are just creeping up to my hips when Isabella finds us.

"Shay! Jules!" Isabella calls. "There you are!"

"Julia and I were just coming," I say.

"You guys go ahead," Julia says.

She doesn't need to tell me twice, and I march off with Isabella right behind me.

I start munching on my snack of cut-up apples before we even get to the portables, and I'm eating them so fast, I start to choke. Isabella pounds me on my back even though we know that's not really what you're supposed to do. Still, I say, "Thanks," once I can breathe again. I'm glad we're far enough away from Julia that I don't have to hear Stacy's donkey laugh.

I sure don't want to believe Hana was right when she said the United Nations might split up, but I can't help worrying, and today worrying feels a whole lot like being mad.

18
Nice

Isabella and I hide from the sun beneath the big magnolia tree. I unscrew the top of my water bottle from my backpack and take a long drink. Momma says if I drink plenty of water, it will help clear up my skin. So far it hasn't made any difference except I do have to pee a lot more, and I miss soda. "Why is it so hot?" I click the bottle against my teeth. But that's not the real question I want to ask. What I want to ask is why Julia is being weird and not hanging with us at break like she's supposed to.

"I know!" Isabella pulls her hair high above her head to cool her neck. She looks like a palm tree. "Ugh, my hair is such a mess when it's hot like this. It's a big frizz ball."

I do not see a bit of frizz anywhere on Isabella's

head. She says her hair is curly, but it's totally not. What it is, is *wavy*. *My* hair is curly. And kinky. And sort of wild. Does Jace like wild or wavy hair? I wrap my hair in a tight knot bun.

"Stop complaining," I say. "You have, like, perfect hair."

Isabella lets her mass of waves plop back down and frowns at me. "Ay Dios mío, what's the matter with you?"

"You sound just like your mom," I say. I don't hear Isabella speak Spanish that much. Usually when she's frustrated.

"I sound like *me*," Isabella says, but then her voice softens. "Seriously, Shay, what's wrong?"

"Nothing," I say. "Sorry." I kick the dirt, and it's so rock hard, not even a tiny bit of dust comes up. "I just . . ." I want to tell her about the makeup and how I'm starting to worry that maybe Jace won't ever smile at me again, but I want Julia to be there too like she's supposed to be. That's the problem with a three-way friendship. When one of us is missing, it's hard to talk about anything important.

But if I say that to Isabella, it would feel a whole lot

like talking about Julia behind her back, and any friend-ship manual you check would tell you friends don't do that. "I want Jace to like me," I finally say. Since Julia already knows that, it doesn't seem wrong to say it to Isabella.

Isabella says, "My mom says women have to speak up for what they want." Isabella's face gets weird after she says that. Like, sad weird. Isabella doesn't talk a lot about her parents, but I'm pretty sure her mom is the one who wanted to get divorced.

"Yeah, right. I'll just walk up to Jace and say, 'Hey! Like me!'"

"I could command you to talk to him," Isabella says, smiling now. She rubs her hands together.

"One." I show her my uncrossed fingers. "I'm *not* playing. And two, that would be totally uncool." I screw the top back onto my water bottle and wipe the sweat from my forehead. It's hot even in the shade. I can't help thinking it wouldn't be so awful if someone commanded Jace to talk to *me*.

"Yeah," Isabella says, and rolls her eyes. "My mom wouldn't say that about a boy anyway. She said I can't go out with anybody until I'm sixteen. And once I do go on a date, she's going to make my tíos come over and have a talk with him." She grimaces. "Scare him away is what she means."

"That's awful!" Isabella's mom likes to remind all three of us to be strong independent women. But having all your uncles come over and scare a guy? Not even Momma would do something that mean.

"Right?" Isabella picks up a seed pod and starts eyeing it. I know she's thinking about a project she could use it in. "Maybe if she didn't hate my dad so much, she wouldn't care."

I don't know what to say to that. Sometimes I feel bad that my parents get along so well when Isabella's parents can't even be in the same room together. When she has birthday parties, her dad isn't allowed to come. I would hate that. "Yeah," is all I can think to say, and then neither of us talks for a minute.

"I don't really care," Isabella says after a while. "I mean about the boy thing. It's not like I even like anybody like that."

"I'm starting to wish I didn't," I say, sighing, and Isabella laughs at that. "Seriously, Is. It'd be easier if it didn't even matter that Jace doesn't think I'm cute."

"What are you talking about?" Isabella asks, sounding shocked. "You *are* cute."

Not as cute as you, I think, which isn't all that cool to think. But then I get an idea. "Hey, you know your green top? The one with the glittery peace symbol?"

Isabella nods slowly.

Of course she knows. It's her absolute favorite. I smile really big because I know I'm about to ask a huge favor. "Can I borrow it?"

"I . . ." Isabella's face looks like she just dusted it with blush. She probably wants to say no. I shouldn't be asking her to borrow it. Not her favorite one. But it's the same color as Jace's eyes, and she looks amazing in it, so maybe I could look good in it too.

"Come on, Is, say yes," I beg.

Isabella twists her hands into a knot, but I know she's going to say yes. She can't help herself.

"Okay," she says, and she smiles but her eyes don't look happy.

It's rotten of me to ask her to borrow it, but she looks fantastic now, so she doesn't need help like I do.

"You're the best! I'll come over after school to get it, okay?" I say.

Isabella nods and I give her a hug, and then the bell rings. "Gotta go," she says.

I watch her run off and wish Julia was there to give me a roller whip. Or to tell me I'm not a bad friend for asking Isabella for her favorite top.

On my way to English, someone grabs my shoulder, and at first I think it's a yard-duty teacher ready to tell me to slow down.

But when I turn around, it's Tyler. "What's up?" I ask him, not working all that hard to hide my irritation. It's not that Tyler is that bad, but he's annoying, and since I already have to put up with him in shop, I don't really need him stalking me outside of class.

"Hey, Shayla," he says, and shows all his tiny teeth. "Um, you don't sit at the basketball courts, huh?"

Since obviously he knows I don't, it doesn't seem like a real question. "I sit with my friends at the lunch tables."

"Oh, cool," he says. "Maybe we could eat lunch together one day?"

As if. "Yeah, sure, Tyler."

He nods happily as if I just said we were going to

go to prom together or something. That boy seriously needs to chill.

"See you in class later," he says, and runs off.

Yolanda is always nice to Tyler, and I don't know how he doesn't bug her. She never even seems to mind when Tyler butts into our conversations in shop. That's being *too* nice.

I think about how asking Isabella for her top wasn't really that nice, especially since I know Isabella has such a hard time saying no. But Hana tells me nice doesn't get you anywhere in this world. All Yolanda is getting out of being nice to Tyler is a big pest. No thanks to that business.

Still, at lunch, I offer Isabella my bag of chips.

"What's gotten into you?" Julia asks, looking at me suspiciously. She knows I like to hoard my chips.

"Can't a friend be generous?" I ask, smiling with all of my teeth.

I hate that Julia didn't hang with us at break. And I hate that Isabella and I didn't talk about it. But we can't talk about Julia behind her back because best friends don't do that, and Julia's still one of my best friends; I just hope I'm still one of hers.

I bet Isabella is hoping the same thing. (She's also probably hoping I don't ruin her top.)

I seriously don't know why Tyler keeps hanging around. You'd think he could take a hint.

19
Book Club

When I ask Momma if we can drive by Isabella's to pick up something, she gets all exasperated with me.

"I have book club tonight," she says.

I shudder. Nothing gets Momma more hyped up than hosting book club.

The guest bathroom has to be *perfect*, and Hana and I are forced to be Momma's prep cooks with lots of dicing and measuring and cleaning up after. You'd think Toni Morrison *and* Oprah were coming over when really it's just Momma's best friends. At least she agrees to swing by Isabella's on the way to the market. (I tell her Isabella has something I *need* for school, which isn't really lying.)

Hana is at Regina's house, so I'm stuck helping Momma all by myself.

She is a terror. I don't know why anyone would care

if the butternut-squash cubes aren't exactly the same size.

When the book-club ladies arrive, Daddy hides in his office and I try to escape to my room, but Momma catches me and tells me I have to come out and say hello.

I like Momma's friends, but they always put me on the spot.

"How're your grades, Shayla?" Ms. Theresa asks.

"You know Shayla can't live with anything less than an A," Momma says with a proud smile in her voice.

"That's the way to do it, Shayla. You'll need those A's when you're ready to apply to college." Ms. Coretta has been talking to me about college since I was five years old. She really wants me to go to an HBCU—that's a historically Black college or university—and I have to keep reminding her I'm not even in high school yet.

"You sure are tall, Shayla," Miss Dee says. (She says this every time she sees me, and just like every other time, I have no clue what to say back.)

"Yes, ma'am," I say.

"Do you have any Black teachers this year?" Dr. Walters asks.

Everyone in Momma's book club is Black, and

they're always asking me stuff like this. Even though I know it's not *my* fault all the times I had to say, *No, I don't have a Black teacher,* it still makes me feel guilty, so I'm glad this time I can say yes. "My PE teacher is Black. She's my track coach too. Coach West is really nice and totally beautiful."

"Mm-hmm," Dr. Walters says. "Figures it would be a gym teacher."

"But she's great!" I say.

Momma gives Dr. Walters a side-eye. "Don't start, Mary—there's nothing wrong with teaching children about fitness and health."

"No, indeed," a few of the other women murmur.

"Track?" Miss Dee says. "You're on the track team, Shayla?"

I prepare myself for humiliating laughter. "Yes," I say, and straighten up tall like Momma is always after me to do.

"Well, go on, girl!" Mrs. Anita says. "I ran track back in my day. Don't be too fast, now, or the boys won't be able to catch you." She laughs and slaps her thigh.

"Now, Anita, don't be filling Shayla's head with your foolishness," Momma says. "You go on to your homework, sugar," she tells me, and she sure doesn't need to ask me twice.

When I get to my room, I pull Isabella's top out of my backpack and hold it up so I can check myself out in the mirror. The green looks good against my brown skin. But will it be good enough for Jace to notice me?

Wearing Isabella's top just might be the thing that finally makes Jace see me as the girl of his dreams instead of the girl with the five-head.

20
Green Tops & Green Monsters

When Jace walks into class, he looks over and smiles, and I smile back really big, then force myself to look away like I don't even care.

All during class, I swear I can feel Jace's eyes burning into my back. When the bell rings for second period, I slowly get my things together so he has time to catch me.

"Hey, Shayla," Jace says.

"Oh, hey, Jace," I say, sounding all casual, as if fine boys talk to me all the time.

"I like that top."

"Thanks." I can hardly breathe.

"Doesn't your girl Isabella have one like it?"

"Uh, I don't—I don't think so." Why is he talking about Isabella?

"Yeah, well, whatever. See ya."

I let out a breath. I focus on the positive. He thought I looked good. That's what he said, right? And he knows my name. And he knows who my friends are—which means he pays attention to me.

But at break I decide not to share this great news with Isabella.

"My top looks so good on you!" she says.

I don't know why, but it bugs me that she calls it her top, even though it is. For today, it's supposed to be mine. "Thanks," I say, but I know I don't sound grateful.

"I can't believe you lent it to her," Julia says. She's decided to hang out with us again at break. I almost wish she hadn't if she's going to say stuff like that. "You really asked to borrow her favorite?" she asks me.

I glance at Isabella. She's leaning back on her elbows and staring up at the sky. "She didn't mind," I quickly say. "She could've said no." That's not really true since Isabella basically never says no.

"It's no big deal," Isabella says, straightening back up. "So, did he say anything? Did *you* say anything?"

"Yeah, he said something," I admit. "He said I looked good today."

Isabella smiles. "Wow!"

"You don't have to sound like that's so hard to believe," I say.

Isabella's eyes get wide. "Sorry! I didn't mean it like that. I think it's great."

"Progress," Julia says, and shoots the trash from her snack into a trash can. "Sounds cool. What else did he say?"

"Not much," I say, and shove a handful of cheesy goldfish in my mouth.

Isabella gives me a big smile, and I feel like one of the little fish is struggling to swim its way back up my throat.

When Isabella runs off to class, Julia says, "You know, Is didn't *have* to lend you her top."

"I know."

"So be nice."

I suck my teeth at that. Julia seems like the last person who should be talking about being nice.

What if Isabella only lent me her top because she knew it would make Jace think of her?

21
Clearing Hurdles

At our next track practice, after we're all stretched out, Coach West tells us what specific events she wants us to train for.

When she gets to me, her smile gets really big.

"The 400," she says, "and hurdles." She holds her hand up for a high five.

I can't leave her hanging, but seriously? Hurdles?

Hurdles take coordination. Why can't I do the 1600 meters? That's like what I do every week. I can manage that. I mean, not *fast* or anything, but I can do it.

I check to see if Angie looks worried. The hurdles is her race, and I just bet she won't want me running in a lane next to her, bumping into her or kicking one of her hurdles over.

As far as I can tell, she isn't thinking about me at all.

Coach West blows her whistle, and we all start practicing.

I try jumping over a few hurdles, but it feels awkward.

"Angie," Coach West shouts. "Help Shayla for a bit. She's struggling with her timing."

I can't believe Coach West called me out like that, and I can't believe she asked Angie to help.

Angie is with the other girls on the relay team: Carmetta, Natalie, and Maya. Our track team isn't all Black, not even close, but the girls' relay team is, and they all exchange glances when Coach West asks Angie to help me. Angie shrugs and Natalie laughs. I wonder what that is supposed to mean. It didn't seem nice.

Maybe I'm doing something wrong, but it doesn't seem like any of the relay girls have any interest in hanging out with me. Hana made that comment about people saying I think I am too good for them, but as bad as I am at hurdles, that sure can't be what's keeping us from being friends.

Angie jogs over and asks me to do a few hurdles so she can see how I'm doing. After a couple of minutes, she stops me.

"You keep jumping with different legs," she says.

"I do?" I look down at my legs accusingly. "Does that matter?"

"Yeah," she says. "You should jump with your lead leg. Your strongest leg. What hand are you?"

"Huh? Hand?"

"What hand do you write with?" She holds up both of her hands, like perhaps I'm an alien from another planet and don't know the meaning of the word *hand*.

"Oh, sorry. I'm left-handed." I think I get it. "So I'm left-legged?"

"Probably. Let me see something."

She gets behind me and then *pushes* me!

I stumble forward and almost fall. "What are you *doing*?"

"People say whatever foot you use to catch yourself, you know, if you get pushed, that's the leg you should use for your lead leg. It's your power leg."

I look down, and my left leg is definitely in front of my right. "Thanks," I say, even though I don't appreciate getting pushed.

"Sure," Angie says with a toss of her braids.

I try jumping over a few hurdles again, this time

making sure I lead with my left leg, and it actually feels better.

Bernard comes over with a small ball in his hand. A shot.

Shot putting, I found out, has nothing to do with guns. A shot looks like a dark softball, and just like a softball, shots aren't soft at all. And they're really heavy. Shot putters have to throw the shot as far as they can.

"Think fast!" Bernard says, and pretends to throw the shot at me.

I flinch, and even though he didn't actually throw it at me, just thinking about that thing flying into my belly gives me a stomachache.

"Bernard!" Coach West yells.

He gets all scowly faced. "What?"

"Do I need to remind you again that the shot isn't a toy?"

"No." He sounds upset.

"Go back to the safe zone with the shot if you're still practicing." Coach West is really serious about her safety rules.

"I'm done," Bernard says.

"Well, then, put the shot away."

Bernard's grip on the shot tightens, and I'm not sure what he's going to do.

"You should put that away," I say.

He turns around fast and glares at me. "You don't need to tell me what I have to do."

"Sorry," I say, my mouth feeling like it's packed with marbles. I shuffle my feet and look at the ground and hope he leaves me alone.

"People always on me," he says.

I don't look up.

"Bernard!" Coach West shouts.

I want to tell her not to make him mad, not when he has that heavy shot in his hand, but he just shuffles over to the equipment locker.

Soon it's time to stack up the hurdles and put them off to the side of the track, and all the relay girls are laughing and joking with each other. Carmetta starts singing a Rihanna song. She has a really pretty voice, and Angie, Maya, and Natalie start singing along. It's one of my favorite songs, and I bet I could sing better than Natalie. She's way off key.

After practice, we all go out to the front of the school to wait for our rides. Whoever picks up Bernard is always already waiting, so he's one of the first people to leave. Maybe it's his mom. I mean, even bullies have mothers.

Groups of kids are scattered all over the grass. I haven't made friends with anyone on the team, so I wait alone. Natalie gets picked up and then Maya. A van pulls up and a whole bunch of kids pile in. Pretty soon, there's just a few of us waiting.

I tell my feet to walk over to where Angie and Carmetta are sitting. It's just the two of them, so I try to convince myself that it's not too scary. But my feet don't listen and my hands start itching and I feel like I'm trapped in cement.

Finally, I convince my feet to get moving and start to walk over, but that's right when Angie and Carmetta's ride gets there, and they both get up and run to the car.

I stare down at my feet.

They have totally let me down.

22
Your Own

That night, I'm standing in the kitchen, keeping an eye on the pork chops so they don't burn.

"Momma, do you think there's something wrong with me?" I start.

"Huh?" She's sitting at the dinner table reading one of her textbooks. This year, Momma decided to go back to school to get her master's in English literature. Momma and I both like to read, but it's a mystery to me why anyone would choose more school if they don't have to.

"I mean, all *your* best friends are Black. And so are Hana's." I feel dumb talking about this. "Is it weird that none of my friends are?"

Momma closes her book and stretches her arms high above her head. "My girls and I have known each other for a long time, Shayla. I guess you could say we speak the same language."

"A Black language?"

She shakes her head. "No, sugar." Then she pauses. "Well, maybe. I mean, not really, you understand, but there's something about those women, my *sisters*, that makes me comfortable. You have to remember, back when I was in school, kids stuck with their own."

"Things haven't changed." I sigh and flip the pork chops. Maybe there *is* something wrong with me. "But I thought Isabella, Julia, and I spoke the same language. At least we used to."

I didn't realize I was stabbing the pork chops until Momma comes over and takes the fork from my hand. "Those chops haven't done you wrong. Why don't you let them be?" She gives me a sideways look. "Shayla, there's nothing wrong with you and your friends. I don't want you to think that's what I meant."

"Julia is really into these other girls all of a sudden. Like she likes them better than the United Nations." I turn to face Momma because I want to make sure she tells me the truth. "Do you think she likes them more than us because Isabella and I aren't Asian?"

Momma shakes her head like that couldn't be possible, but then she says, "I can't speak for Julia, Shayla. But even if it is true that she likes those other girls because they have something in common with her that you don't have, that doesn't mean she likes you and Isabella any less. And it doesn't take away from the friendship you girls had."

I can't help notice Momma said *had*, like maybe we don't have it anymore.

Momma puts the chops on the cutting board so they can rest, and checks the rice. "Shayla, do you *want* to have Black friends?"

"I don't think they want to be friends with me." It doesn't sound right, saying it out loud. "It's like since I don't sit at the right place at lunch, I'm different or something." Not one of the girls on the relay team seems interested in being my friend. Angie's nice to me but she's nice to everybody.

Momma gives my arm a little squeeze. "Nothing wrong with being different. And right now, you're just becoming who you're going be. You still have a lot of growing to do."

Momma must know I'm about to interrupt, because

she holds up her hand to stop me. "Trust me. You're going to change in all sorts of ways. That doesn't mean there's something wrong with you, Shayla. Or with the friends you have. Just make sure you're open to all sorts of people. Now, I will tell you this. You may find as you get older that there's something . . . comfortable, or I don't know, comforting, in having friends who can relate to things you might be going through. Little things like knowing what type of product to put on your hair, and big stuff like knowing how it feels when we hear about the police hassling someone just because they're Black. Or worse than hassling. That *hurts*. Those are things Julia and Isabella might not relate to. Although I bet they have their own things." Momma chuckles, but not in a this-is-so-funny way, in a sort of sad way. "That doesn't mean they aren't your friends, or that you should feel bad about those friendships. You hear me?"

I nod. It's a lot to process. And I think maybe part of what she is saying is that I really need to get some Black friends.

"But I'll tell you this too. I've met a really wonderful woman at school who I like a lot. We've started running the stairs together on campus, and even though I haven't known her as long as my other friends, I think she and I speak the same language too."

I don't know what this has to do with anything, but then Momma says, "Janice isn't Black. She's white."

Hana walks in just then and throws her hand against her chest like she's having a heart attack. "Daddy, come quick! Momma is starting to fraternize with white folk!"

Momma swipes at her with a dish towel, and that makes Hana laugh, and I feel a little bit better.

A wise man once said (okay, it was Michael Jackson): "It don't matter if you're Black or white." But obviously, MJ didn't go to Emerson or have the police stop him for a busted taillight. Race shouldn't matter, but it does. For real.

23
Black Panthers

I'm beginning to think I was wrong to worry about the United Nations being in trouble. Julia has been around almost every break for the past few weeks. I try not to think her missing break time with Isabella and me every once in a while is that big of a deal. And of course she's *always* around at lunch.

Like today, it's just us three like normal, laughing and joking and being silly, until Isabella asks about Halloween costumes.

"Bruuuuuh," Julia says, sounding like a frog. "Costumes are for babies."

Isabella, Julia, and I always pick a costume to do together. One year we all dressed up as sand castles and had glittery sand in our hair (and other uncomfortable places) for days. Another time, Isabella and Julia were two parts of a table, and I was the gum stuck underneath them. "You don't want to dress up?" I ask.

Julia gives a funky little snort (which is very unattractive) and looks at me like I'm *so* yesterday. So I take that as a no.

When I get home after school, I ask Hana if it's cool to wear a costume in junior high, and she says I should if I want to, like that is the important thing. She shows me the big afro wig and gold hoop earrings and Black Panther T-shirt she is going to wear. Most people hear *Black Panther* and they think of the movie, but Hana is quick to remind everyone the activists came first. Hana's dressing up as Angela Davis. Hana shows me pictures of other people who were in the Black Panthers, and when I see the black jackets and berets, I think I have a good costume idea. I can dress up but not look like I'm way over the top. And a beret will cover some of my forehead. Sold.

I don't bother with Julia, but I convince Isabella she should dress up too. We decide to surprise each other with what we're wearing. I can't help but hope Isabella doesn't wear something that makes her even more beautiful. Maybe she'll be a scary witch. With a wart.

•••

On Halloween, I put on Daddy's black leather coat, which of course is huge on me, but that's okay, and then a black beret Momma got in Paris. She says she bought it even though no one was actually wearing them there because it made her feel French. She also tells me I better not lose it. But once I have the coat and beret on and check myself out in the mirror, it doesn't seem all that exciting. Then I get a great idea. The one thing about Halloween is, I can get away with wearing makeup since it can be part of a costume.

Hana walks into the bathroom just as I'm putting on mascara.

"Shayla!"

I almost blind myself with the stick of mascara. I guess I should've asked her first before borrowing her makeup.

"Did you see anybody wearing makeup in those pictures I showed you?"

I wipe the black smear off my face. "That was a long time ago. Probably now they would wear it."

Hana sighs loud. "You're supposed to be a *protester*. I know it's just for Halloween, but can't you even take a second to think about how important protest is? How it's not about looking cute?"

I totally want to call Hana out because she looks fantastic as Angela Davis and I doubt she minds. But I'm smart enough not to say it.

Hana stands there for a couple more seconds and then walks away.

I put on some green eye shadow.

On the way to school, Momma keeps giving me little sideways looks until finally I say, "What?" She probably is thinking I shouldn't have makeup on.

"Just seeing you dressed that way," Momma says, "makes me . . ." She shakes her head. "Seems like we keep protesting and nothing changes. My daddy got arrested for protesting when he was just a little older than you. And look at us today. Same stuff going on. This trial . . . Mm, mm, mm." Momma shakes her head again. "I thought we'd be in a better place by now."

I feel bad I'm wearing something that makes her sad, but when we pull up in front of Emerson, before I get out of the car, Momma says in a big voice, "What do we want?" Even though she's sort of shouting, she's smiling.

So I smile back. "Justice!"

"When do we want it?"

"Now!" I shout back at her, giggling. She gives me a kiss goodbye and tells me to have fun.

"I will," I say, and climb out the car.

There's a bunch of people in costume, and that makes me feel less nervous about dressing up, but seeing so many people in costume makes me wish the United Nations had come up with a costume idea together like we used to.

Jace isn't wearing a costume, and I worry that means he'll think I'm a big loser for dressing up. I push my beret down lower and smile at him, hoping mascara is making my eyes look bigger. I just need him to notice *one* time my forehead isn't as big as the moon.

Today doesn't seem to be the day.

Mr. Levy has his hair brushed back nice and neat, and he isn't wearing his lab coat. His costume is being normal. Hilarious.

"We're going to howl like banshees!" he tells us in this excited way he gets sometimes.

He passes around a bowl of nuts. Not the eating kind, but the metal kind that sit at the end of a screw. And then he passes out balloons. The whole time most everyone is already howling. And Mr. Levy doesn't stop us.

He tells us to each put the nut in our balloons before we blow them up. When we swirl our balloons around, they make weird, squeaky noises. I'm not sure if that's what a banshee sounds like, but it's super loud.

Bernard swings his balloon so wild, he hits the boy sitting next to him, who acts like Bernard punched him or something. I'm pretty sure a balloon wouldn't hurt that much, but Mr. Levy sends Bernard to the office anyway.

I don't think Mr. Levy likes Bernard.

Today's a minimum day, so each class is shorter, which means I get to meet up with my friends at break earlier than usual. But when I get to our spot, only Isabella is there.

Her long hair is in two braids, and she has a bright yellow flower pinned on one side. Her top is white and it's a little off her shoulders, and then she has a bright skirt on that's full of flowers and birds. She looks amazing.

"You look great," she tells me. "What are you dressed as?"

"A protester. From the sixties. The Black Panthers?" Then I force myself to say, "You look awesome."

Isabella spins around. "It's from a painting. I really like the artist, Mia Roman Hernandez? She's Puerto Rican, like me."

"Oh, cool," I say, even though I've never heard of this Mia person.

"I don't look stupid?" Isabella asks, fiddling with her braids.

I can't believe Isabella doesn't realize how fantastic she looks. "No," I say. "You definitely do not look stupid."

"Where do you think Julia is?" Isabella asks. I'm pretty sure I know, but I don't say. Isabella shrugs. "Guess she got held up in second period."

"Yeah, maybe," I say. *Or she wants to stand around and laugh at every dumb thing Stacy says.*

I wonder if Julia will be sad when she sees that Isabella and I dressed up. Especially since everyone in costume gets a special pass to eat lunch on the front lawn.

It's weird to think I probably won't see Julia at all today.

• • •

When it's time for lunch, Isabella and I meet up out front instead of the lunch tables.

The front of the school is nice, with a big hill of grass and trees and flowers and stuff. Normally it's off limits for lunch because there's no gate, and I guess they think kids would just wander off.

A sculpture of a guy's head sits right in the middle of the grass, and when Isabella and I go over to look, I see that of course it is Ralph Waldo Emerson. He looks pretty grim. Maybe I should have dressed up as him for Halloween; that would've been scary.

Coach West comes over while I'm reading the engraving on the plaque below the statue. It lets me know Emerson lived from 1803 to 1882, and it says:

OUR GREATEST GLORY IS NOT IN NEVER
FAILING, BUT IN RISING UP EVERY TIME WE FAIL.

I think about that for second. Honestly, if I have a choice, I'd pick not to fail.

"Interesting man," Coach West says. She points to the quote. "No one really knows if he's actually the one who said we should get up after we fail, but I'm guessing he would've thought it was true. He believed an easy life doesn't teach much."

"I guess," I say.

"Sounds like my mom," Isabella says.

Coach West chuckles at that. Then she says to Isabella, "You look like you walked right off of Mia's canvas," and Isabella grins real big. Then Coach West looks me up and down. "Huey Newton? Bobby Seale?"

I'm not surprised Coach West would know my costume is for one of the Black Panther activists. Even though I didn't know those names before Hana told me, I nod happily.

"You should enter the contest," Coach West tells us, and nods toward a row of benches.

The student council is having a costume contest, and if you want to be in it, all you have to do is join the people waiting for a turn to walk across the benches Student Council lined up like a runway. Isabella giggles and I rub my itchy hands together and say, "No, thanks."

"Okay, well, have fun," Coach West says.

Isabella and I find a spot on the pokey grass, and just as I'm rearranging my beret for the millionth time, I see Julia.

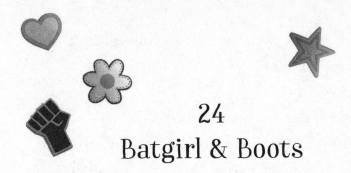

24
Batgirl & Boots

Julia's dressed as Batgirl, and let me point out there's no way anyone could come up with that costume at the last minute. But that's not the worst part.

All her other friends are dressed as superheroes too.

I can't even *believe* Julia did a group thing with them and not with us. I can't even believe she didn't tell us. I can't even.

She comes over and plops down like it's no big deal. "So, Shay, what exactly are you supposed to be?"

I don't want to answer her. I don't want to talk to her. I pinch my wrist to keep from saying anything.

"Huey somebody?" Isabella says. "A protester from a long time ago, I think."

"Ooooh," Julia says. She picks a wish flower from the grass and blows it. I want to tell her you're not supposed to do that. It's just spreading weeds around. "Yeah, I get it, bruh," she says, nodding. "On the real." Then she stands back up.

I look up at her and shield the sun out of my eyes so I can see her better. I have a ton of questions sitting fat and slimy on my tongue that I want to spit out.

"Nice costume, Jules," Isabella says, and even though Isabella doesn't say it in a mean way, I think all three of us know there's a lot being said right there.

Julia's cheeks get a little pink, "Hey, you want to hang with us?" she asks.

"No thanks," I say, barely opening my mouth to get the words out.

Julia just stands there for a second like she isn't sure what to do, but then she says, "Okay, then, late!" and runs back to her other friends.

This is another new Julia-ism. Instead of saying, *I'll see you later,* like a normal person, she shouts *late* at you, like she is too busy to be bothered with adding the *r.* She even does it in text messages.

I can't tell if Isabella is as mad as I am. I've never really seen her get upset over anything unless she's fighting with her little brother. She's just too nice to call

Julia out, and the reason I didn't say anything to Julia is because if I said one word, a whole bunch of other ones would've come out.

And Momma tells me all the time not to say anything you can't take back.

I watch Julia and Stacy whisper together and then crack up laughing, and my belly pinches tight.

"She acted like she wasn't going to dress up," Isabella says. There's a question tucked in Isabella's voice. She starts sucking the end of one of her braids.

I don't say anything.

Isabella's eyes are big and sad, and that makes me even angrier. "I guess she changed her mind," Isabella says.

I don't say anything.

"Well, she looks great," Isabella says with a little sigh.

"But she acted like dressing up was dumb," I complain.

"She must've decided it wasn't." Isabella shrugs. "And we dressed up anyway."

"That's not the point," I say. "Doesn't it make you mad?"

"I wore what I wanted. Didn't you? Besides, maybe it was a command," Isabella says.

"Is!" I start in, but a darkness blocks out the sun.

Bernard.

He has a patch over one eye, which seems less like a costume and more like he got into a bad fight recently. He must've had it in his backpack, because he wasn't wearing it this morning in science. I can't believe an eye patch is a ticket to the lawn. And I can't believe when I'm feeling like punching somebody, Bernard is over here bothering me. Obviously, I can't punch *him*. I look over at Julia and then away quick. I don't want her to think I'm worried about her at all.

"Hey," he says. His voice isn't just really loud, it's also really deep.

"Oh, hey, Bernard," I squeak out. I glance at Isabella, wondering if she's on the verge of freaking out too, but she doesn't seem bothered.

"Hey," she says to Bernard.

Bernard glares at me, but I don't think I've done anything wrong. Maybe he just wants to sit in this spot. The grass is scratchy, so I wouldn't mind leaving if he wants us to. I don't have Bernard figured out anymore. I know if he wants something, he'll just take it, but at the same time, he doesn't act all that mean to me. Still, I can't help but feel afraid every time I see him.

"I want to sit here," he says, and plops right down.

Isabella and I exchange looks again. This time her eyes are wide like mine.

Great. We are in the space he wants. At least he didn't shove us out of the way or anything.

I look around to see if Coach West is still around. She'll step in if something's about to go down. I know Bernard isn't doing anything wrong, but my brain can't keep adding *yet*.

"Sorry," I say, and get up. "We were just waiting for the contest line to die down." I grab Isabella's hand. "So, come on, Is, let's go."

"Fine," Bernard says, frowning at me.

Once we are in line, Isabella asks, "You really want to enter the contest?" She sounds surprised, because it's not the type of thing I would normally do.

"We have to now," I say. "Bernard freaked me out. It's like he's after me."

"Drama queen? It doesn't seem like he's *after* you. And anyway, he doesn't seem *so* bad now." Isabella adjusts her flower.

"You haven't seen him when he's mad." As soon as I say it, I feel guilty because *I* haven't really seen Bernard acting all that mad recently. (Snatching Legos when we were in second grade probably shouldn't count.) But he did break that slide. And knocked over his desk. And whacked someone with a balloon. It's not *my* fault he's scary.

We slowly move up in line, and my stomach starts doing cartwheels.

Isabella goes first. And she walks down the runway of benches like it's no big deal.

I take a couple of steps on the first bench. I had no idea it was going to be so wobbly! I take another step and start to slip. I wave my arms to catch my balance. I look ridiculous, and the only thing I can think to do is try and turn my wack moves into a dance, and so I wave and slip and *groove* my way across the benches.

I hear Coach West shout out, "Go, Shayla! Go, Shayla!" and then Bernard says it too, with his deep booming voice. And then it seems like everybody is shouting at me to go.

Gladly, I think.

I've thought of Bernard as a bully for so long, it's hard to think of him any other way. Maybe Isabella is right and he's not so bad. But I still know better than to make him mad.

If I had dressed up as a superhero, I would have been Atom Eve, with those cute pink boots. That would have been cool.

25
Black Power

After fifth period, on my way to shop, I run right into Principal Trask. Like, literally. She turned the corner the same time I did, and *wham!*

"Sorry!" I say, and try to rush off, but she stops me.

She looks me up and down and frowns. "Young lady, do you really think it's appropriate to wear that to school?"

I look down at myself, because I don't know what she's talking about. "This?" I've seen girls in ridiculously flashy, slinky costumes today that seem inappropriate, but there doesn't seem to be anything wrong with what I have on.

"Yes. Glorifying such a violent time in history . . . such a violent movement." Principal Trask shakes her head. "Just doesn't seem like a good idea, does it?" She tips her head to the side, waiting for my answer.

My mouth goes dry, and my heart is pounding so hard, it feels like someone's beating it like a drum. And my hands are on fire. "But—" I want to say how the Black Panthers weren't about violence, but my mouth won't cooperate.

"Maybe you should take it off," Principal Trask suggests, almost as if she's being helpful.

I'm not sure if she's actually telling me I have to, and I sure don't want to. But no way can I get into principal-level trouble. Momma would kill me.

"Okay," I finally say. I slide the beret off my head and wriggle out of Daddy's coat. Luckily, under that I have on regular stuff. Just a black T-shirt and black jeans.

Principal Trask looks me over. "That's better, right?" she says, and actually almost smiles at me like we're pals now or something. Principal Trask isn't good at smiling. "And watch where you're going." She sniffs and brushes past me.

I head to shop, feeling awful. I don't think my costume was bad, and it sure wasn't supporting violence. Momma never would've let me wear it if that had been true. And I hate how Principal Trask wanted me to agree with her that my costume was a bad idea.

When I get to class, my sour mood must show all

over my face, because Yolanda asks me right away what's wrong. She's dressed up as Princess Leia, and her hair is in those two huge buns.

When I tell her, her eyes go wide. "That's not fair."

"I know," I say.

"Wait, Trask made you take off your costume?" Tyler says, butting in. "I thought it was cool." He sticks his fist up. "Black power!"

I don't want to say she didn't actually *make* me take it off. Maybe I shouldn't have. "We weren't talking to you," I tell him, and Yolanda frowns at me. I'm being a tiny bit rude, but he's being majorly rude for just busting into a conversation he wasn't invited to.

Tyler laughs like I said something nice. "Yeah, my bad."

"She's just in a bad mood because of Trask," Yolanda explains to Tyler, and he nods.

"Cool. Cool," he says. "Talk to you later."

When he walks away, Yolanda sort of hisses at me, "That was rude."

My eyes widen in surprise. "I don't think he even notices."

"He has feelings," Yolanda says. "*Everybody* does."

"Okay, okay," I say. "Sorry."

26
Squad Goals

When Momma picks me up, she asks me why I'm not wearing my costume.

"It got too hot," I say. I don't want to tell her about Principal Trask because I bet Momma would get heated about that. All I want to do now is go home and figure out how to waste time until trick-or-treaters start showing up.

I'm in that weird in-between Halloween stage. Too old to go out and get candy, and too young to go to the kind of parties Hana goes to. Hana and her friends have "old school" parties. Everyone goes to someone's house, and they play a lot of music and dance. Sounds fun.

Isabella thought that maybe we should go to Fright by Night at Six Flags. I didn't even have to ask Momma if I could go. A big N-O is what she'd have to say to that. I don't mind too much because walking around in the dark with zombies and monsters jumping out at you is not my idea of a good time.

Sometimes I wish I could be more like my friends, but it sure seems like being brave gets people in a heap of trouble. And just thinking about that makes my hands itch.

It's not so bad being stuck at home tonight. I get to pass out the candy, and the kids who come to our door are the cutest. I've seen about twenty Wonder Womans and a whole slew of minions. Spies are big this year too, and a little girl in a tiny trench coat and dark sunglasses is absolutely hilarious.

I take some snaps and send them to Is and Jules. Our group chat started when we all got phones last year. It's pretty cool that I can scroll all the way back to those old messages. We don't have nearly as many messages this year.

Isabella is sending updates from the horror-movie marathon she's watching. It's the only way I want to see a scary movie. Her saying, *Oh no, she doesn't see the mean doll moving behind her* is enough to give me a tiny heart attack. Julia only texted once, to say she ate too many Reese's Pieces and then a snap of her with a silly Halloween filter.

By nine o'clock our porch light is off. Momma says

she doesn't want any big kids knocking on our door that late, and she tells me it's time for bed even though I'm not even a little bit tired.

I snuggle into my flannel sheets and flip through pictures on my phone. I'm not really supposed to use my phone after nine, but it's way too hard to try to sleep when you're not tired.

My phone buzzes with a message from Isabella.

Isabella: Check out Stacy's posts.
Me: You're friends with Stacy?
Isabella: I follow her online. I follow everybody!

I have a bad feeling, but I find Stacy's profile and click on the first post. It's a picture of her and Julia and a few other girls. In their superhero costumes at Six Flags. I flip through more pictures. They're at Westwood. At someone's house swimming. At the movies. Each picture gets me more upset. I can't explain it. It's not as if I didn't know they were friends, but seeing Julia's smile like that—her really, *really* wide one, that she only does when she's having the best time ever—makes me feel bad. And she must think there's something wrong with these pictures if she didn't post them on her own profile.

Stacy makes a new post, and this one's a video. And even though I want to shut off my phone and not look anymore, I click the volume so I can hear them, and they are screaming like zombies are about to chew off their faces and then they all shout, "Squad Goals!"

Seeing that makes my eyes tear up.

And then my bedroom door bangs open and there's Momma filling up the doorframe. "Shayla? What are you doing?"

I slide my phone under the covers, hoping to hide the glow.

Momma isn't stupid. "I know you're not texting after nine o'clock."

This is Momma's way. To tell you she knows you're not doing the very thing you are doing.

"I'm . . . I'm . . ." I wipe my nose and blink back tears and hope I look as sorrowful as I feel. Maybe Momma will understand.

"Hand it over, Shayla," Momma says, holding her hand out.

She can't mean it. She can't. "Momma, I'm just—"

"Shayla," she says.

What can I do? I hand her my phone. So basically my life is over. Momma doesn't understand at all.

27
Density

Without my phone, I'm completely cut off from the whole world, and Momma is obviously mad at me. I can't even enjoy Saturday and Sunday.

After such a lousy weekend, it is no surprise that Monday starts out bad too.

My favorite jeans are still in the dirty-clothes hamper, and all there is for breakfast is banana yogurt.

I'm in a funk the whole way to school. I pulled some hair out of my usual sloppy bun, and straightened it, to have side bangs. I thought it would be a distraction from my forehead, but the style bugs me now. I pulled out too much hair, so the bangs are too long and my hair is starting to frizz already. I bet I look like an emu.

When I get to science, I scrunch down in my seat and wait for the day to be over.

"New lab partners today," Mr. Levy announces, and starts calling out names.

I don't bother fantasizing, because where did that get me last time?

Then something amazing happens.

"Shayla and . . . Jace."

I have to bite the inside of my cheek to make sure I don't make a squealy sound. I peek back at Bernard and he scowls at me.

After Mr. Levy explains the lab, I saunter back to a lab table, where Jace is waiting, as if I couldn't care less that we are partners. But the closer I get to him, the bigger my smile gets. He smiles right back at me. My heart gets as big as a horse. Seriously, I have a huge stallion stomping around inside my chest.

For the lab, we have to pour different substances into a big beaker to test for density. We both reach for the honey at the same time and our hands brush.

Then a few minutes later, there is this one moment when our heads get really close together. Thank God I brushed my teeth real good this morning!

At the end of class, before I can get out of my seat, Bernard puts his heavy paw on my shoulder.

"Hey, Shay," he booms.

I try to get up, but Bernard has me trapped.

"I have to get to second period, Bernard."

"Maybe we'll get to be partners again." He gives my shoulder a squeeze.

I bet I'll have a bruise.

28
Highlights

At break, Isabella *and* Julia are at our spot behind the portables, and at first all the bad feelings from Halloween come rushing back, but I push them way, way down. I decide it's not right for me to be mad that Julia and her friends went to Six Flags when I didn't even want to go. I still want to ask her about dressing up with her other friends, but I don't want to mess with the good feeling I have about Jace.

He'll probably be my boyfriend soon. I know better than to tell Isabella and Julia that, though. They'll say I'm being silly.

I do feel silly, but silly-good. Like my smile spreads out to my elbows, and even my knees are happy.

"Are you okay?" Isabella asks.

"Yeah, it's just . . ." I'm going to hold on to this

feeling in private. "My mom caught me using my phone late and took it away." That definitely wipes the goofy smile off my face.

"Oh, that's rotten," Isabella says, and she and I exchange glances. I'm sure she knows why I was using my phone late.

"So that's why you didn't answer my texts," Julia says. "I thought you were just bent." She flings her hair back, making it easier to see her new blue highlights.

I can't even get mad at her for trying to talk like she's so *down*, and copying Stacy's highlights. Me and Jace are lab partners now and he *smiled* at me. *Twice*. That wipes away a whole heap of bad feelings.

I drift off to PE thinking about Jace's green, green eyes and wide smile. Even though he jokes around a lot, he's not really a *smiley* person, so I don't think I'm being ridiculous to think him smiling at me means something.

I feel like I swallowed electric butterflies and they are lighting up and swirling all around inside me.

After the mile in PE, Yolanda says, "You sure do like running." Her hair is twisted together on both sides, and she is huffing and puffing like we had to run two miles. "You smiled during the whole mile."

"Really?" I ask, giggling into my hands. We walk to the water fountain together, and I wonder if I could trust her with my secret. Even though we have two classes together, we never talk about important stuff. Would she think I was being ridiculous if I told her about Jace?

"Hey, how come you're always so mean to Tyler?" she asks all of a sudden.

"I'm not trying to be mean." I know I was rude to him on Halloween, but I was in a horrible mood. "He is always bothering me, though."

"He's just being friendly. You should cut him some slack."

I've noticed that Yolanda is sort of like Isabella. Nice to everybody. I don't think I'm a mean girl, but I'm definitely not as nice as they are. "You should tell him to leave me alone." I'm only joking around, but Yolanda gets a stern expression like I'm one of her little brothers or sisters acting up. She told me she has to be on them all the time.

But then she smiles at me, flashing her upside-down Y. "Seriously, Shayla. He's not so bad."

"Okay," I say, but I'm not sure what I'm agreeing to.

When I get to shop later, I do try and be nice to Tyler, but he's sort of like a puppy sitting under the dining table. If he gets a tidbit of food, he's just going to beg constantly.

So I don't snap at him when he gets me my shop gloves; I just say, "Thanks." Yolanda rolls her eyes, and I want to tell her to make up her mind.

When the final bell rings, I just about fly out of class so I can get to track practice. Those wild butterflies are back in my belly, and I can't wait to start running so they will go away, or at least they'll get tired and relax.

I can run a mile easy now. I run and focus on putting one foot in front of the other, and I keep going when my side pinches and my breathing sounds like a saw chomping on stacks of wood and my hair gets hot and heavy.

Running makes everything bubbling around inside twist and turn and spread out behind me like wings. Julia hanging with her other friends trembles at the tips of my wings before twisting away into the wind. The butterflies from Jace's smile escape from my belly into the air and fly away. Yolanda wanting me to be nice to Tyler scatters and whirls around me like a pile of brown and orange leaves. I don't worry about anything; I just run.

And then it's time to practice the hurdles.

29
Timing

Even though I always use my lead leg now, I'm still not getting over the hurdles easily. Because, *hello*? It's HARD.

Coach West says my long legs will really be an advantage once I get the timing down, and I don't want to call her a liar, but . . .

Sometimes getting over hurdles seems impossible. The only thing fun about it is when all the hurdlers line up and do high kicks. It's supposed to limber us up, but it feels like dancing in a chorus line. Too bad it hasn't made it easier for me to jump over the hurdles.

You have to jump with your leg (your lead leg) sticking straight out like you're doing some flying kick into somebody's stomach, which should send you sailing right over the hurdle. My jump right now doesn't look a thing like it is supposed to; it's more like a hop-leap-stumble.

At least I have running clothes now.

"Shay!" Bernard barks at me, right when I'm going over a hurdle, making me trip over it.

I dust off my skinned knee, and I'm too angry to worry about Bernard being so much bigger than me. I stand up and my hands go to my hips. "What?" I ask, and I don't ask nicely.

"Did you ask Mr. Levy to change partners?" Bernard walks up to me until he's right in my face, and I have to take a step back.

"No!" *That never would've worked.* "Why would you think that?"

"You seemed really happy about it."

My anger seeps out of me like a leaky balloon. "Oh," I say. "That's just because I liked the lab. It was fun, wasn't it?" This is a dumb question, because Bernard definitely didn't have fun with the density lab. He and his new partner, Rebecca, spilled olive oil all over their table, and then before they finished the lab, Bernard knocked their whole beaker over so they never actually got to put any findings into their lab books.

"It would've been fun if we were still partners." He walks away with his head sort of down.

I almost want to run after him, but I don't know

what I'd say. I like having Jace as a partner now. I dreamed about it. I can't tell Bernard that.

I also can't seem to get the hurdles down, and it's getting so frustrating.

Angie makes it look so easy.

Coach West watches as I struggle to get over the hurdles. I bet she's thinking she made a big mistake assigning me to that event.

A hurdle trips me up, and I tumble to the ground. Maybe a track made of recycled tires is softer to run on, but it still hurts when you fall on it.

I climb to my feet and rest my hands on my knees, breathing hard and trying to keep the burn behind my nose from becoming tears.

After practice, Coach West tells us all to huddle up. "We won't have a real meet until track season starts, but I thought it would be good for our newcomers to see what a meet might feel like." She smiles at me and my mouth goes dry. "So I've invited Oak Junior High out for a preseason meet. It'll be fun. And we have two whole weeks to get ready for it."

Coach West is smart, but she doesn't know what she's talking about. A practice meet does not sound like fun. And two weeks isn't nearly enough time.

30
Face Plant

Today is the preseason track meet. Everybody in the whole school is here (that's what it feels like, anyway). Posters have been up for days advertising it, and each time I saw one, I wanted to tear it down. The kids from Oak seem way too hyped up considering this meet doesn't even count.

I line up for my first race—the 100-meter hurdles. My stomach is aching in that crampy way that means I'm about to get my period, and my palms itch so bad, it's like fire ants are biting me.

I rock back and forth in the blocks to get myself ready and take a deep breath before settling in. When I hear one of the coaches from Oak call, "Set," I make sure I don't move anymore and just wait for the starting pistol.

There's a moment right after set is called when it feels like the world stops. As if everything alive holds its breath. Blood pounds in my ears, and my mouth goes dry.

When the starter pistol pops, I take off, thinking, *Okay, okay, this is going to be great.* I go over the first hurdle, easy as pie, just like in practice. I take one step, then another and another, and am over the next hurdle, then I'm not counting steps, I'm just going, and I sail over the third hurdle and it rattled down when I hit it, but no big deal, that happens all the time, and then here comes the fourth, the fifth and then it is a bit of a blur, and then BAM! I'm flat on my face with a hurdle on my back.

The sixth hurdle, to be exact.

I am probably going to die. Or maybe I'm dead? Except I hear laughter coming from the stands. There are times when I hear people laughing and I think they're laughing at me, but really they aren't. This isn't one of those times.

Coach West comes over and helps me up. "Happens all the time, Shayla. All the time. Don't let it break you."

I feel broken into so many pieces, I can't figure out how to put myself back together. I slowly get to my feet, dust myself off, and start to limp off the track. I figure people won't laugh so hard if they think I've twisted an ankle or something.

"Shayla, where are you going?"

"What? I'm, I'm going to sit down." I stop when I see the surprised look on Coach West's face.

"You still have a race to finish. You're not hurt, are you?" She is asking, but I can tell there is only one answer.

I look down the track. The rest of the girls have finished, of course, and now it is just Coach West, the track, four more hurdles, and me. "I still have to finish?"

"Don't you want to?"

I start to shake my head, because no, I do *not* want to. But there is something about my coach's expression that stops me. I can feel sweat beading up on my forehead (that's a lot of sweat).

"Trust me, Shayla. You should finish. You really should." She leans forward and her whistle glints in the sun. She gives me a little pat and then whispers to me, "Get up every time you fail."

I don't care if he's the one who really said it or not, right now I sort of hate Ralph Waldo Emerson. I turn back to face the enemy and start limping my way toward the seventh hurdle. At first the stands seem scarily quiet. And then I hear Julia shout, "Yaaas, Shayla!"

As I jump/stumble over the remaining hurdles, I can hear people cheering, and I feel for a second like one of those football players who go down for a hard hit, and everyone's worried that he's paralyzed or something, and then he gets up and the crowd goes wild. It isn't exactly like that, but at least I'm able to smile when I cross the finish line.

Coach West comes running up. "See? What did I tell you?" She beams at me, so I smile back at her. But then she says, "You still have the 400. Are you going to be able to run it?"

I gulp. The last thing I want to do is run another race. "Um . . . I'm not sure. My ankle doesn't feel great." I bend over and rub my ankle. Coach West just smiles and pats my shoulder before running off to deal with some other runner. I bet she knows I'm faking.

I head to the grass in the middle of the track, and Angie comes over and sits down next to me.

"You all right?"

I'm sure Coach West sent her over to check on me,

but it still feels nice for Angie to be sitting next to me like we're friends. "Yeah, just a little . . ." My voice trails off, and I rub my ankle some more. I wish I had one of those long Ace bandages to wrap around it. That would totally make me look too hurt to run.

"That was a hard fall," she says.

I just nod. The grass is crunchy beneath me and scratches my legs.

"Must've been embarrassing." She stretches her right leg in front of her and bends over it to touch her toes.

"Totally!" For some reason, saying it out loud makes me feel better, and I smile.

"I've fallen too. No biggie. Everybody falls doing hurdles."

I can't imagine Angie ever falling.

Angie switches her legs around to stretch her left leg. "You were doing good up until then."

"How would you know? You were blazing way ahead of me."

"True." Angie does this thing I've seen her do when she smiles and looks just like a cat about to catch a big bird. It's a sneaky and proud smile.

"You're really good at hurdles," I say.

"You're getting better," Angie says. "You and the other newbies are working hard. I bet you were definitely going to finish at least fifth." Angie gives me a soft punch on the shoulder to show she's just kidding around.

"Oh, *thanks*." I nudge her with my shoe. "So there I was running as hard as I could, *losing*, and then, wham!" I laugh.

She laughs too. "It was kind of funny."

"Are you saying you were laughing at me?"

"*With* you," she says and gives *my* foot a nudge. "And you got up and finished. That was great."

"I guess. Coach made me feel like I had to," I admit.

"But you didn't have to." Angie pauses for a minute. "So you ready for the 400?"

Now I'm positive Coach West sent her to talk to me.

I don't answer. I'm feeling good now; why ruin it?

31
Bounce

Before I can figure out what I'm going to do, Bernard is standing there looking down at me. *Oh great,* I groan to myself.

"You okay, Shay?" he asks.

"Yeah, I'm fine," I say.

"I thought you were going to win," he says.

"Thanks!" Angie says sarcastically.

Bernard blinks a few times, looking back and forth between me and Angie, and then he grins like he is just getting the joke. A smiling Bernard looks just the same as a scowling one.

Angie stands up and offers me her hand. "We gots to go, big boy. Have to get ready for our next events. Right, Shayla?"

"Yep," I say.

When we are out of earshot of Bernard, Angie bumps into me. "Looks like you got someone crushing on you."

"What?" I almost trip over the grass.

If she had said Bernard wanted to crush me, I would've believed that. But *crushing on* me? Like he likes me? That is almost scarier.

We find Coach West and tell her I'm good to go. She doesn't even look surprised; she just turns to Angie. "So what are you doing here? Don't you have a long jump to do? Scoot." Angie gives me a thumbs-up and runs off to the sand pit.

"Okay, Shayla, they're lining up for your race," Coach West tells me. "Just stay loose, okay?"

She smiles at me like she actually thinks I can do that. But no part of me is loose. I think even my blood is tight.

I clench my teeth. When I get to my spot, my palms start itching. I rub them together, but that doesn't help— it never does.

The gun pops, making me jump.

I try to find a nice steady pace, but I feel like a mangled robot, all out of sorts and jerky. As I round the first bend, I almost stumble. Wouldn't *that* have been nice? By the time I get to the straightaway, I'm in fifth place but closing in on the girls right ahead of me, and I decide, what the heck? So I push myself as hard as I can and pass the girl ahead of me, then I close in on the girl who had been ahead of *her* and then, and then . . . I finish fourth.

Isabella and Julia give me high fives after the meet.

"You were great, Shay," Isabella says.

"You fell with so much grace," Julia says, and giggles. "You got *style*!"

"Shut up," I say, but I giggle too.

Still laughing, Julia adds, "Sorry, my bad."

That makes me laugh harder. Then Isabella starts. And it feels like old times, the three of us laughing at something that isn't even funny.

Julia says in a rapping, singsong voice, "Today you took an L, but tomorrow you bounce back."

Isabella sings, "Bounce back. Bounce back."

The three of us do this bounce move we made up. It's pretty great having friends who can make you smile even after something awful.

And then Stacy comes over, and my smile dribbles away.

164

"Nice face plant, bruh," she says.

And Julia laughs. She laughs instead of telling Stacy not to be a jerk. And the laughter doesn't feel at all like it did just a minute ago.

I still think not failing in the first place has got to be better than getting up after you fail.

I never knew laughter could sound so different and feel so different depending on who's doing the laughing.

32
Everybody Dance Now

Now that it's been a while since that awful practice meet, people have stopped teasing me about how "gracefully" I fall. Alex, of course, still thinks it's spectacularly funny to pretend to trip almost every time he sees me, but his goofiness doesn't bother me today, because it's the last day before winter break. Two whole weeks off! We don't go back to school until after the first of the year, and to celebrate, there's a dance in the gym.

Even though Julia has been saying how dumb the dance will probably be, I'm excited. Maybe I'll get to dance with Jace. He hasn't thrown any more smiles my way, but at least we're still lab partners.

The doorbell rings and I run to get it.

Isabella's mom is dropping Isabella and Julia off so we can all go to the dance together, and afterward they're both sleeping over.

The sleepover will be just like old times, and I'm probably more excited for it than the dance. It's weird at school now, because ever since Halloween, Julia hangs out with her other friends at break a lot instead of me and Isabella. She calls them her squad. Isabella and I pretend it doesn't bother us, but I'm sure it hurts Is's feelings just like mine. At least Julia still sits with us at lunch.

Mrs. Álvarez comes to the door to say hi to Momma.

I love Mrs. Álvarez. She is always telling the three of us how strong we are—which is all kinds of hilarious considering what a softy Isabella is. Her accent makes her sound like this movie star Momma likes, and Mrs. Álvarez actually looks like she could be a movie star. I guess I shouldn't have been so surprised when Isabella turned out to be hiding a whole bunch of beautiful under her unibrow and braces.

Momma and Mrs. Álvarez chat for what seems like forever, while Isabella, Julia, and I make funny faces at each other. We can't go off to my room yet, because Mrs. Álvarez needs to give Isabella a lecture first. It's their thing.

Mrs. Álvarez gives Momma a hug, and then she starts in on Isabella. I don't actually know what she's saying because she's talking in Spanish, but I can tell by her tone, and by Isabella's face, that it's definitely a lecture. At the end of it, though, her mom gives her a big hug. Maybe Mrs. Álvarez is really a big softy just like her daughter. "What are we going to do with these girls?" she asks Momma, and they both shake their heads and sigh, and I'm sure we're going to hear all about how tragic it is that we're growing up. Luckily, this time, Mrs. Álvarez just gives Isabella a quick kiss.

"*Adiós,*" she tells us. "Be good."

Finally, we can escape to my room.

"What did your mom tell you?" I ask Isabella.

"Not to dance too close to any boys. Not to dance too . . . you know." Isabella starts dancing sort of wild, making me and Julia crack up. She spins so out of control, she makes herself fall, and I give her a hand, helping her back up. She smooths down her dress and adds, "And she said to stand up for myself. She thinks I don't do that." Isabella doesn't look at us when she says that last part.

"Next time she tells you to clean your room, say *no*. And then when she gets mad, tell her you're just standing up for yourself," Julia jokes.

Isabella and I just shake our heads at Julia.

"We all look so cute," Isabella says. All three of us

got our dresses from the same rack at Kohl's, so we're dressed pretty much the same. It's not exactly a fancy dance, but we know enough to dress nice.

Julia snaps pictures of me and Isabella, and then Isabella pulls out her phone and takes more. We all crowd in together to take some selfies.

I wish I had my phone so I could take pictures too. "Let me see them," I ask Julia, but she nudges Isabella.

"Show her yours," she says.

As I flip through all the pictures, I notice how plain I look next to my friends. "You guys are so lucky you get to wear makeup," I say. They only have on eye makeup, but I'm still jealous. Isabella's is faint, just a swipe of shiny bronze, but Julia's is bright sparkly blue. It doesn't seem fair that my friends have different rules about makeup.

I wonder if Hana's advice about sneaking makeup to school (something I haven't tried) applies to school dances. I think about Jace being there and how great Isabella looks, and I think about how I still don't have my phone back, so it would be really stupid to get in trouble . . . and then I end up putting some of Hana's eye shadow, mascara, lip gloss, and blush into my purse. Not that many girls carry purses in junior high, but I got my period back in elementary school and got caught one day without any "supplies." It was super embarrassing to have to ask the school secretary to help me out. Now I always have a purse when I don't have my backpack.

In the car, Julia scoots close to me and asks in a loud whisper, "You gonna ask Jace to dance, Shay?"

"Yeah, right." I cut my eyes at her.

"Who?" Momma asks, peering at me in the rear-view mirror before focusing back on the road.

I knew she would pick up on some boy mention.

"Nobody, Momma," I say.

"And this nobody is called Jace? What kind of name is that?"

"Momma!"

"I'm just saying . . ." Momma taps her fingernails on the steering wheel and doesn't say anything for a few minutes.

I should've known she was just loading her ammunition.

"Now let me tell you girls something," she starts, and I bite my sigh way back. "All three of you are too young to be fooling around with boys. Plenty of time for all that."

"We know, Mrs. Willows," Julia says in her best, I'm-the-sweetest-most-obedient-child-ever voice.

"You all *better* know," Momma says.

"My mom tells me the same thing," Isabella says.

When we get to the gym, kids are lined up outside, waiting to get checked in. Momma lets us out of the car and says, "I'll be back at ten."

I'm so happy she isn't chaperoning, I almost start dancing right there. But I don't.

Once we get inside, we head to the bathroom so I can "freshen up." My eyes look bigger with eye shadow and mascara, which does seem to make my forehead look smaller.

We get drinks from the snack table, and I look around for Jace. I don't see him anywhere.

Then Julia's squad comes over and grabs her, pulling her onto the dance floor with them. So much for it being the three of us.

Isabella and I start dancing with each other. My head bops to the music, and I swing around, but that's not part of my dancing; I'm keeping an eye out for Jace. It never occurred to me that he might not even come to the dance.

Boys shuffle around the edges of the room. Must be hard to be them. They can't just dance together like girls can. That doesn't make a lick of sense.

And then suddenly, there's Jace, and I feel like maybe I have asthma or something because it's hard to breathe. He starts dancing right next to me. The makeup must've done the trick!

But then I realize that although he is dancing next to me, he is actually dancing *with* Isabella.

It feels like somebody just dumped a bucket of ice-cold water on my head. I stop dancing and walk back over to the snack table.

A minute later, Isabella joins me. "Hey," she says. "You left me." She's a little out of breath.

I look back at the dance floor. "Where's Jace? I thought you guys were dancing?"

Isabella picks up a tiny cup of pretzels. "He was just dancing next to us, Shayla, and then—"

"I know what happened. I was there." I eye the snack table. Pretzels, goldfish, cookies. It all looks terrible.

"Then why'd you walk off?" Isabella asks, munching on a pretzel.

I can't believe she can eat at a time like this. "Why do

you care?" My voice sounds all trembly, and that makes me mad. "Isn't he a good dancer? You should've kept dancing with him. He obviously wanted to dance with you."

"But . . ." Isabella stops and looks down into her cup, like the great excuse she might have for dancing with the boy I like might be hiding in there.

Someone touches my elbow.

"Hey, uh, Shayla, you wanna, um, dance?"

I know who it is before I turn around. "Hi, Tyler," I say. And only because I'm mad and don't want to stand next to Isabella right now, I say, "Sure."

The gym has gotten crowded with kids dancing, and Tyler pulls me right into the middle.

All of a sudden, a group of boys runs up shouting, "Command! Command!" at Tyler. I forgot about the stupid game. I cross my fingers quick even though I'm not playing. I don't think Tyler has anything crossed, but he doesn't look worried.

If that wasn't a huge clue, my itchy hands should've been.

"We command you to kiss Shayla!" Paul Childress crows.

"But I'm not playing!" I yelp.

"So, Tyler is," Paul says. "If he doesn't kiss you, we get to pound him."

I've never liked Paul.

"Yeah, um, sorry," Tyler says.

I can tell he isn't sorry AT ALL. My face is blazing.

33
Chapped Lips

Before I can say anything, Tyler kisses me. I'm not talking a peck on the cheek; his mouth is *smothering* mine.

I don't really have a lot of kissing experience. Okay. I have *no* experience. But I sure know this isn't a nice kiss. It is slobbery, and even though he must've just had a mint so at least his breath isn't bad, his lips are chapped and scratchy. I'm so busy analyzing it, I don't pull away in a hurry like I should, and instead just stand there, mouth locked with him.

A whistle blows, and then Coach West breaks us apart.

"None of that. None of that." She looks sternly at us, and I want to crawl under the floor. Then she blows her whistle one more time and walks away.

Tyler runs off, laughing and high-fiving his boys.

I feel like I've gone way up high in the Sierras or maybe up in a plane, like my ears are totally clogged up and I can't hear and my head is heavy.

"Shay!" Isabella says, dashing over to me. "What was *that*?"

"It was just a command!" My ears won't pop, and my voice sounds like I'm under water. Maybe it's all the tears that feel like they're gurgling around in my throat.

"I thought you weren't playing," Isabella says. "Why didn't you say no?"

"Like you know all about saying no, Is," I say. My head hurts like someone is squeezing it. I want to sink into a hole.

"Why are you mad at *me*?" Isabella asks, all shocked as if she really doesn't know.

I'm not sure what to tell her, but before I can tell her anything, Bernard is standing next to me, asking me to dance, and the night is officially the worst ever.

"Fine," I tell him. I'd rather dance with Bernard than admit to Isabella I'm mad that she's so pretty and Jace danced with her.

Bernard frowns at me while we're dancing. He bites

his lip, then opens his mouth like he's going to say something, then closes it again. Finally, he asks, "I saw you with Tyler and all. What's up with that?"

I step to the left. I step to the right. I snap my fingers and turn around. I do not want to talk about that kiss anymore or ever, ever again.

"Are you guys talking, or what?" Bernard barks at me. "Because I . . . I . . ."

I can't tell if his expression is angry or sad, so I shrug his question away. I shrug like it's a dance move I just invented. Angie telling me Bernard might have a crush on me wasn't any type of good news. If I tell him me and Tyler aren't talking, does that mean *he's* going to try and talk to me? And how could I tell him I'm not interested without making him mad?

Bernard says, "That's cool," as if I have actually answered him. But he doesn't sound like he thinks it's cool. "You like him?"

No. But Momma says (and says, and says) if you don't have anything nice to say, just keep your little mouth shut. Saying I don't like Tyler seems mean. "Uh, Tyler's nice," I say.

"Dang" is all Bernard says, but it's enough. Enough

for me to realize I'm pretty dumb not to have noticed that maybe Bernard does like me a little. And maybe hasn't wanted to punch me. And maybe . . . a shudder goes up and down my back . . . maybe if he had thought of it, he might've had someone command him to kiss me. We don't talk for the rest of the song.

34
Double-Crossed

I tell Bernard I need to use the bathroom, but I really just want to get away so he won't ask me to dance again. Before I can find a dark corner to hide in, I end up walking right into Julia and her squad.

Stacy starts giggling when she sees me, and she gives Julia a little shove. "Jay, you said she'd never do it!"

Julia's face gets red.

"Bruh, you should totally thank us," Stacy says to me.

Julia gets even redder and elbows Stacy.

"*Thank* you?" I ask. Stacy's face is all smirky and Julia's is all embarrassed, and I get it. "It was *you*? You guys got Tyler's friends to make that command?"

Julia's now redder than the spiciest hot wings. "It was just a joke, Shay!" she sputters. "Don't get it twisted."

"Right? Besides, you guys make such a cute couple," Stacy says, sounding like she's the couple expert. "Didn't I tell you, Jay?"

"We do not!" I glare at Julia.

"Why'd you kiss him, then?" Stacy asks.

"I didn't!"

"Sure looked like it," Stacy says. "I thought you liked him."

"It was a command and you know it." My hands go straight to my hips, and I'm so about to let Stacy Chin have such a big piece of my mind, it'll flatten her, when Julia gives my elbow a tug.

"It wasn't that big of a deal," she says.

"It was to me! How could you do that?"

"I thought it would be funny?" Julia says, her voice lifting at the end like she's not really sure.

My eyes start to burn. "Friends don't do stuff like that, *Jay*." I'm not sure why it bugs me so much that her other friends have a different nickname for her. "So not cool."

Stacy looks back and forth between me and Julia. "Bruh, seriously, we didn't even think it would go that far. It was just a joke." Lynn and the other girls behind

Stacy look very uncomfortable. "My bad. And I was just messing around about the couple thing."

I'm not nearly as mad at Stacy as I am at Julia. Julia's my best friend. She should've known how uncool it was to set me up like that.

"Sorry," Julia says. She gives me a little nudge and I nudge her back but harder. I'm mad. Like, really, really mad.

"Where's Is?" Julia asks, trying to change the subject.

Being so mad at Julia makes me feel nervous about how I treated Isabella earlier. I probably owe her an apology. This is turning into one sorry night.

Julia glances around and I see her face change. "Oh, uh, she's over there," she says.

I turn to the dance floor.

I know by the expression on Julia's face what I'll see. The heat in my neck goes all the way to my scalp, and it feels like my ears finally pop. The music and laughter around us sound too loud, and yep, there's Isabella and Jace. Dancing and laughing and looking like a great couple.

35
Sorry Sleepover

A slow song comes on and I think the long rope of intestines inside me is tying up into one huge knot. I am stuck watching Jace and Isabella like I'm playing freeze tag. I don't want to watch, but I can't look away.

Jace looks like he is trying to talk Isabella into dancing, but she shakes her head and then looks around, and even though I'm sure she's looking for me and Julia, I push my way through the crowd and go over to an empty corner of the gym. I want to be alone. I can't believe a minute ago I was trying to find Isabella so I could say *I'm* sorry. I used to think I was super lucky because some people only have one best friend and I had two. But what do I do when my two best friends have both done me dirty?

The bottom row of bleachers is pulled out, and I sit

down and stare at the crowd of laughing, dancing people and want to bury my face in my hands.

The slow song ends, and a good fast song starts. Lots of people start singing along to the song and throwing their hands up.

Isabella finds me, and she has Julia with her. Great.

Isabella says, "Come on, let's dance all together. Just the three of us."

"Yeah," Julia says. She holds her hand out to pull me up, but I don't take it.

"No," I say. "I don't want to. You guys go ahead."

Julia drops her hand, and then she and Isabella stand there for a few seconds. I don't know what I want them to do, but it isn't Julia saying to Isabella, "Let's go."

Isabella raises her eyebrows at me. "I want to dance some more before it's over."

"I'm not the boss of you." My voice comes out louder than I want.

"Fine, Shay," Isabella says, and now she sounds annoyed with me, which is all kinds of ironic.

My friends leave me with my salty attitude and join a big group of girls dancing together.

After a while, the lights start flashing, and parents

come in to take their kids home. I'm so through with this dance. I stand up and head for the door. Momma is right on time, and I'm glad to see her. That's because I forgot about my makeup experimentation.

I remember quick when I see how Momma is looking at me.

I open my mouth to say something, but nothing comes out. I look down at my shoes and wish I could disappear.

"I'm sorry," I finally say.

"Let's go" is all she says.

Probably because she is mad at me, she doesn't notice how upset I am. I stay next to her as we walk to the car, neither of us saying anything, while the setter-upper and the boyfriend stealer walk behind us. I'm not sure if the sleepover idea is such a good one anymore.

Climbing into the car, Julia whispers, "Are you in trouble?"

I'm so upset, I can't say anything.

"I should take you two girls straight home," Momma says. "Shayla does not deserve company tonight." Her hands are super tight on the steering wheel, and my stomach feels like hot rocks are rolling around inside.

"But your mothers are expecting you to be with us, and I don't want to mess up any plans they might have."

I swallow hard, trying not to cry. I wish I could tell her that I don't even want them to stay over anymore.

As soon as we get home, Momma says, "Shayla, go wash your face."

Getting ready for bed, Isabella and Julia act like the only thing that's bothering me is getting caught wearing makeup. It makes me feel even worse, because shouldn't my friends know why I'm upset?

I try and pretend everything is okay because I don't want to ruin our slumber party. Julia takes a few selfies of all of us and I fake-smile. Maybe this is how Isabella feels a lot of the time. Not letting herself get mad. It's not a good feeling, and I can't keep all my hurt feelings from bubbling right out. Maybe if Jace hadn't seen me kissing Tyler, he would've wanted to dance with me.

As we line up our sleeping bags, my smile slides off my face. It feels like finally taking off a pair of too-tight shoes. "How could you have done it, Jules?"

"What?" Julia asks, pretending she doesn't know what I'm talking about, and acting all innocent. Then she looks down at her phone instead of answering me.

"Done *what*?" Isabella asks.

"Julia and her *squad* were the ones who set up that whole command." Julia plotting with her other friends makes me feel like she is picking them over us. Over *me*. She probably wishes she was sleeping over at Stacy's.

"Seriously?" Isabella asks. "Jules, that is *so* not cool. No wonder you were mad at the dance, Shay." She turns back to Julia. "You know how Shayla feels about Tyler."

"It was supposed to be funny, Is!" Julia says, instead of denying it. "Can't you two chill?"

"I would never have done that to you," I tell Julia.

"Chill *out*, bruh." Julia taps something into her phone and grins at it. I'm sure she's being super funny with her friends. "You didn't have to go along with it."

"I'm not a bruh, *Jay*."

"But Tyler is," Julia says, and snorts like she's hilarious. She still isn't looking at me. Instead she's focused on her phone, and I almost snatch it away from her.

"Not funny," I say.

"For real," Isabella says.

"Okay!" Julia says. "Sor-ry."

Anybody can tell you that's no way to apologize. And she sure doesn't seem all that sorry, the way she's just clicking away.

"Is, check out all the snaps," Julia says to Isabella. "They're hilarious." I know she's just trying to change the subject, but it still makes me mad, especially when Is picks up her phone and starts looking at pictures too.

I wonder if it is too late to ask Momma to take them home. "Are you two seriously going to be on your phones all night?"

"I was just looking at the pictures. You want to see them?" Isabella holds her phone out.

I do, but for some reason I say, "No, thanks."

Isabella nudges me with her toes. "That was messed up that Julia did that," she says. "But you kind of seemed mad at *me*." Her voice is quiet, and I can tell she wants to ask me something, but I pretend not to hear her.

I yawn extra wide. "I'm exhausted," I say, and flop down on my pillow.

The room is quiet except for the sound of Isabella's and Julia's tap-tap-tapping. Obviously they aren't texting me. I turn on my side, away from them.

36
Nothing Good

In the morning, I wake up before they do. Julia's phone is next to her head.

I bite my lip, considering. Momma says nothing good ever comes from peeking where you're not supposed to, but I can't help myself. I pick up Julia's phone. She has it password protected, and for a second I worry that with all the other changes, maybe she changed her password too, but it's the same 0213 it's always been. (That's her birthday.)

There's a bunch of group chats with her and her friends, but the first message is one from Isabella. It's just two sad-face emojis. So, of course I click on the thread to see what Isabella is sad about.

Julia: You got to dance with Jace!

Isabella: Shayla said I should've danced with him,

like she didn't care.

Julia: Do you like him too? He's SO cute!!!!!
😊 ♥ 😊 ♥ 😊 ♥

Isabella: He IS cute.

Julia: You should go for it. Yolo, bruh.

Isabella: Shayla would probably get mad. 😟

I don't know what to think, and I want to stop reading, but I can't. Isabella is right that I would be mad, so I don't get why they kept talking about it.

Julia: She doesn't have dibs or anything. It's not your fault if he likes you.

Isabella: 😟 😟

I stare at the faces. Is she sad because she is being a horrible friend or sad because she cares about my feelings?

I set Julia's phone down. I climb back into my sleeping bag and pull it way over my head.

When we all get up later, Momma makes banana pancakes, which is what she always makes for the three of us. This morning, they taste like sand. Momma asks Julia and Isabella what they're doing for winter break.

It's like she's trying to fill up the kitchen with noise since I'm being so quiet. Julia says she has a basketball tournament, and Isabella talks about an art camp she's doing. I don't say anything.

Momma keeps giving me side glances, trying to tell me with her narrowed eyes that I'm being rude, but I can't force a smile onto my face. Julia and Isabella go pack their stuff up, and I'm super glad when Julia's mom comes and picks them up. As soon as they're gone, I give Momma a hug.

I need a hug bad. I swallow hard, trying to push the stinging tears down.

Momma lets me hug her for a minute, and then she untangles my arms from around her waist.

"Shayla, we have talked about makeup before, so I *know* you know better."

I nod without looking up.

"Do you want to explain why you thought you could break the rules?"

I fiddle with my fingers. There's no excuse that is going to save me. "I just wanted to look special," I admit.

"Well, you didn't look special. You looked like a girl

trying too hard. And I know there's a boy mixed up in here somewhere."

"I—" I stop myself from saying anything that will get me in more trouble.

"I've done told you, Shayla, you don't need to be messing around with any boys. See how it already got you into trouble?"

I feel horrible because I got into trouble for no good reason. Jace didn't even notice that my eyes were bigger. "I'm sorry."

"I'm sorry too. Yes, indeed. You don't get to decide the rules. Your daddy and I do." Her voice is like tiny knives piercing me.

"I know!" It comes out angry even though how I really feel is like a used-up tissue.

"Excuse me?"

"I'm—I'm sorry, Momma. I won't do it again." It is hard talking over all those salty tears stuck in my throat.

"No, you won't." She stares out the window for a few minutes, and I know she's trying to figure out my punishment. "Okay, Shayla. We don't need to talk about this anymore. But don't think you're getting your phone back anytime soon." She pauses, and then she adds, "And don't make plans with your friends over winter break. I have some extra chores for you to do."

"Yes, ma'am," I say.

When I go back to my room, I sit on my bed thinking about the dance and the kiss and my friends and just how horrible everything is.

Used to be that people would ask if it was hard having two best friends. Now I know that what's really hard is feeling like you don't have any friends at all.

37
BD/AD

Mr. Powell explained that world history is divided into two sections: BC (before Christ)—or some people say BCE (before the Common Era)—and AD, which stands for *anno Domini*. That's Latin for "in the year of the Lord." Well, now *my* history is divided into two sections: BD and AD. Before Dance and After Dance.

BD, I was excited. I was stupid enough to believe that if Jace *really* saw me, he'd see I was his soul mate.

AD, I'm pretty sure I don't want to see Jace or hear his name ever again, especially if his name is anywhere near Isabella's.

BD, Momma was smiling at me and acting like I was growing up.

AD, she throws away the makeup I used (even though it was Hana's), grounds me, and looks at me like she is thoroughly disappointed. (My parents know disappointment hurts a lot more than anything.)

BD, I was looking forward to winter vacation. I figured it would be relaxing and fun.

AD, I realize there is nothing relaxing about thinking of all the fun you are *supposed* to be having.

At least I'm filling up my eyeball journal. Since the dance, I have pages and pages of "observations." I have to make sure Julia and Isabella never read it.

Usually when our house phone rings, it is someone trying to sell something. But since I don't have a cell phone, Isabella and Julia have been calling the house phone. I don't talk to either one of them. Momma will come into my room with the phone, and I'll just shake my head. She thinks I'm trying to punish myself, but I figure it's still just someone trying to sell something, and I'm not buying.

Yesterday, Momma asked me what is on my Christmas list. What I actually want is a smaller forehead and friends I can trust. I don't think Santa will be bringing me either of those.

Sometimes when I'm in a bad mood, all I want to do is stay there, and maybe live in pj's and eat gummy worms. Unfortunately, Momma gets in the way of those types of plans. That's why I find myself at the mall, trailing behind her as she finishes her Christmas shopping. She says she refuses to let me mope, like moping is such a bad thing.

I sigh through Macy's while she looks for a sweater for Daddy, grumble through Forever 21 as she searches for earrings and jeans for Hana, and drag my feet through the lingerie section of Sears the whole time Momma tries to find a nightgown for Mama Dear.

"Shayla! That is it! Here's five dollars. Take it and your sorry attitude to Starbucks and wait for me there."

"Fine."

BD, Isabella, Julia, and I would've had lots of fun hanging at the mall, listening to Christmas carols blare from loudspeakers, and skating on the fake ice rink—it's really for little kids, but we love flying around on it, crashing into each other. We do it every year. Did it. Used to.

AD, I watch tight groups of friends giggle past me, and moms with strollers and huge shopping bags order up caffè americanos and skinny vanilla lattes.

I sip my decaf caramel macchiato, feeling absolutely lousy.

38
Spoonful of Sugar

"Hey, Shayla! How's it going?"

Coach West grins down at me. Her arms are loaded with colorful bags, and she has on this really pretty red sweater and a long, black swooshy skirt. She looks like a magazine ad.

It is *so* weird seeing Coach West in regular clothes, shopping at the mall like a normal person. I guess even teachers need to do holiday shopping. "Hi, Coach," I say. Even seeing my favorite teacher isn't going to get me out of a bad mood.

"Mind if I join you for a minute?" she asks. "I've been shopping all day, and I think I'm at the dropping part now." She doesn't wait for an answer; she just collapses into the seat across from mine. "Whoo. What a relief." She stashes her bags around her. "Enjoying your break so far?"

"Yeah, it's okay," I lie. What am I supposed to say?

"Really? Because you sure don't look like everything's hunky-dory."

Hunky-dory? "Oh, well, I . . ." Coach West sets her elbows on the table and leans forward like she actually cares. "I sort of have some friend issues right now," I say.

She nods like she totally gets it. "Yeah, friendships can be tricky. Especially when you change schools. And you all are getting older, so that can be hard too."

"But it's not even about that! No matter how old we get or where we go to school, our friends should still want to be with us, and they shouldn't backstab us, or try to steal boyfriends."

"Boyfriend, huh? That guy I saw you getting up close and personal with at the dance?"

"No!" I hate that stupid, stupid Command game! "That was just a stupid . . . uh, dare." I don't care if the Command game is ended forever, but I'm not going to be the one to tell on anybody.

"Dare? I know kids are going to do all sorts of silly things, but don't ever kiss anybody you don't want to, okay?" Coach West sounds super serious, and I hope she's not mad at me.

"I won't," I say, and boy, do I mean that!

"Good. But, so if not him . . . ?" Coach West lets the question stretch out in the air between us. I can almost see it.

My face feels too warm, and it isn't from my hot drink. "Well, he's not really my boyfriend." Now, *that's* an understatement. "But I like him. And he likes my friend instead. And it's like she doesn't even care. She probably likes him back and they'll just . . ." Now I am the one letting my words just sit there in the space between us.

Coach West nods. "When I was in junior high, my best friend was so gorgeous, and I was just this tall, homely girl with pimples and braces." She takes one look at my disbelieving face and adds, "*Really.* How many guys want to go out with a five-foot-eleven beanpole? With bad skin?"

I know Coach West just wants me to feel better. I bet she's always been beautiful.

"It was some wild twist of fate that Monique and I were best friends. She was so beautiful. She still is, actually. And all the boys liked her. At least that's what it felt like. But then there was this guy." Coach West gets a goofy little grin. "Albert. He wasn't all that cute, but he was smart like me and *funny*. He was short but I didn't care. I liked him. And he was nice to me, so I thought . . ." Her grin goes away and she gives a little shrug. "Of course he liked Monique. And I couldn't really blame him. I would've liked her too. She was also nice, if you can believe that!" Coach West gives her pretty laugh.

"That's awful!" I say.

"But I did blame Monique. Like she had been pretty on purpose. Just to hurt me, you know?"

Boy, do I know.

"I stopped talking to her. I acted like a real butt, if you want to know the truth."

"Did they start talking? Her and Albert? Or . . . um, go out?"

Coach West laughs. "I know what *talking* means, Shayla." She laughs again, but then her smile gets a little bit sad. "No, she wasn't interested in him at all."

"Exactly! That's what a good friend—"

"Oh, I don't think it had a thing to do with me. Maybe it did. But it was more likely the fact that Albert was sweet, but sort of . . . nerdy? He would've been perfect for me if he had only realized it." She chuckles.

"But the point is, Monique never did anything wrong except look the way she did. And what did I want? For her to put a bag over her head?"

I have no answer. Would I be happier if Isabella got her braces back on and let her eyebrows grow together? A tiny bit of me would be happier, but I know it's a stinky green jealous part.

"I don't like giving advice, mainly because people so rarely take it, but you know crushes can be like . . . fairy dust. Special and sparkly and sort of magical, but then most times, they sort of blow away. And if you've gotten rid of friends just to chase the dust, well then, you don't have anything." She opens one of her bags, and I'm certain she is going to pull out that bottle of sugar Mary Poppins carried around to help the medicine go down, but instead she pulls out a bright purple scarf. "Do you think Mr. Powell will like this? It's a little electric, but purple is his favorite color."

"I guess so," I say. Some kids make jokes about Mr. Powell's scarves, saying they're girly. I hate when people talk bad about him. And who cares if he likes to wear bright colorful scarves? He's an awesome teacher. "Yeah, for sure, he'll like it," I say.

"Great. He can be so hard to shop for. Well, thanks for letting me sit a spell," Coach West says, gathering her bags together. She gets up from the table and pats my shoulder. "Merry Christmas, Shayla. Try to have some fun. We'll be practicing hard for track once school's back in."

"Merry Christmas," I say, my voice coming out in a tiny croak. I want to call Isabella right then and apologize, but I don't have a cell phone.

I still have half a drink left but I get up and throw my cup away.

When Momma finds me a little while later, I tell her we need to leave.

I'm so ready to dump this awful feeling. As soon as I get home, I'm going to call Isabella.

39
Silent Protest

When we get outside, there's a large group of people chanting and holding up signs, blocking our way. A woman with a megaphone is yelling about justice. I've never seen so many angry faces. And even though I know none of them are mad at me, it still feels scary to be surrounded by all that anger and yelling.

Momma grips my hand.

"No justice, no peace!" a bunch of people shout.

A loud crash makes me jump. Someone threw a rock through a store window, and I squeeze tight to Momma. I'm not used to feeling so small. Like I'm getting swallowed. Everyone is jostling and trying to get closer to the entrance of the mall, and Momma and I can barely get through.

This is the first time I've seen a protest up close. On the news it seemed like it would be exciting, but this is scary. Someone shoves me, and it makes me lose my grip on Momma's hand. "Momma?" I shout. I look around and don't see her. Just a sea of frowning faces. "Momma!" I call again.

And then she's there, grabbing my hand. "Come on," she says, just about yanking me through the people to get to the parking lot.

We crunch over the glass covering the sidewalk.

Momma and I rush to the car, but after she shoves her bags in the trunk and we climb into the car, she just sits there without turning on the engine.

For a few seconds all I hear is both of us breathing hard.

Then she turns on the car and we pull out of the lot. Police officers are arguing with the protesters and a tall man with dreads has his hands handcuffed behind him.

"He's getting arrested?" I've never seen someone in handcuffs except on television.

"I guess they think he's the one who broke that window."

I chew on my lip, not knowing what to say.

Momma tunes the radio to a news station. I hear a bunch of confusing trial talk.

"What are closing arguments?" I ask.

"It means they're close to the end," Momma says. "With the protesters outside, I thought maybe the verdict had already come out." She wipes sweat off her forehead.

"You thought she was found innocent?" I can't keep the shock out of my voice.

Momma doesn't answer, which is the same as saying yes.

"But that won't happen, will it?" I ask.

"No one knows, baby. But I know folks are starting to worry. And that makes them scared . . . and angry."

When we get back home, I don't know what to do with myself. I don't feel like calling Isabella anymore. I don't want to do anything, really, except sit in my room and feel miserable. That protest was awful, and the trial isn't even over. I can't imagine how bad it will be if the police officer is found not guilty.

Hana busts into my room without knocking. "Stop moping around," she says. "It's driving everybody crazy. There's too much going on in the world for you to be acting like some big baby."

"I'm not!" I shout.

"*Excuse* you?" Hana says, taking a step forward like she's going to punch me.

"Fine," I say. "Sorry."

She comes all the way into my room and sits next to me on my bed. "Junior high is the worst. Trust me, I remember. But that doesn't mean you can ignore everything else."

"I'm not, Hana. It's just . . . Momma and I saw a protest." I gulp thinking about it. "I don't want that officer to get off, but everyone was so angry, and someone broke a window."

Hana nods. "Yeah, me and Regina were talking about how bad things are getting. There was almost a riot at the last Black Lives Matter rally when a bunch of people started shouting against us. But stuff like that can make it seem like our movement is just about spreading violence."

"Are we about violence?" I don't want the answer to be yes. Even though I know we have plenty to be mad about.

Hana doesn't answer right away. She looks angry, but Hana usually looks like that, so it's hard to know what it means. "No," she finally says. "But it can be hard to stay calm when sometimes it feels like . . . like people don't care about us. Or act like they have to be afraid of us. Or maybe want to control us." She adjusts her ponytail and looks like she's thinking hard.

"When a Black person gets shot and nothing happens, it's like we don't matter. And that makes me angry, and yeah, it makes me want to do something violent. Make some noise. Get *attention*. I want a scholarship to play ball next year. It's not fair that I have to take some schools off my list because I would be afraid to live there. I don't know if a lot of white students have to worry about that."

It's the first time I've seen Hana look more scared than angry. It makes the whole thing with Julia and Isabella seem not all that important, which I guess was Hana's point. "I guess I have been a little whiny," I say softly. I bite my bottom lip. I wish I had a big eraser that could just wipe away all the bad feelings.

"It's okay," Hana says, bumping me with her shoulder. "I probably whined a little at your age."

Hana stares at me for a second, tapping her fingers together, and then she says, "Hey, you want to come with me? To a rally at UCLA?"

"Do you think it'll get violent?"

"I don't think so. Not this one. This one is special. And I think it's time you started seeing what all this is about."

"If Momma will let me," I say.

"Let's go ask," Hana says, and we both go to find her.

"I don't know," Momma says at first.

Daddy puts his arm around her shoulders. "I think it's a good idea. In fact, I think we all need to go."

In the car, Hana tells us it is going to be a silent pro-test. I'm not sure what that means. Seems like if we want anyone to pay attention, we have to yell and scream. But that's because I didn't know there are all different sorts of noise.

Daddy parks in a big parking garage, and when we get out of the car, I see him and Momma exchange looks back and forth. Momma comes over and grips my hand. It reminds me of when I was little and we'd walk to the library or be in the market, and she'd hold my hand so tight, making sure she didn't lose me.

Hana gets a sign out of the trunk. It says *Stand with Us or Stand out of the Way*. She hands me the sign I made that says *We Matter!* over and over again in a bunch of different colors and with glitter sprinkled all over. I'm really proud of it.

We start walking to Westwood, and all I hear is cars swooshing by.

Even though we haven't met up with the other marchers, it's like we're already doing the silent protest, because no one says anything, but we're walking pretty fast.

We turn the corner, and there's a whole bunch of people. Holding candles and signs.

Hana is like a pro. She knows right where to go for us to get candles, and then she has us stand with the big group, and she does it without saying anything. I don't get a candle because I have my poster in one hand and I'm gripping Momma with my other one.

My cheeks are cold, but I brought gloves, so my hands are warm.

And then we start marching. We fill up one whole side of the street. Cars that want to go by pass us really slowly.

And no one says a word.

That's when I find out how loud silence can be.

Hundreds of people walking together, carrying candles and signs but not saying one single word? Let me tell you, that's louder than anything.

There are posters of Trayvon Martin and Philando Castile and Alton Sterling and Michael Brown and

Tamir Rice and Stephon Clark, and a bunch more people who lost their lives. Too many. I get an awful lump in my throat, seeing those faces. Most of them look really young.

Momma keeps wiping away tears and squeezing my hand tight.

A few people honk their horns at us, but I'm not sure if they're on our side or against us. Some people shout, "All lives matter!" and I know they're against us. For real.

I keep looking at those posters of the people who got killed and looking at my daddy, and my mouth goes so dry, it's like trying to suck dirt.

Not all the people walking are Black—not by a mile—but it's still the biggest group of Black people I've ever been with, even counting our big family reunion in Atlanta last summer.

Although it's for a sad reason, and there are a lot of angry faces, it feels good to be part of something. To belong.

Lots of police officers watch us, and I wonder if they feel sad about the posters too or if they are angry at us for marching.

Some news reporters are there, but every time they try to stick a microphone in someone's face, the person just waves them away.

When I was in first grade, our teacher would have us play the Silent Game. We had to see how long we could go without saying a word. Now that I'm older, I know she was just trying to have a few moments of peace. We never stayed quiet for too long. Something about not being able to talk always gave someone the giggles, but tonight it's not hard to stay quiet, and for sure I don't feel like giggling.

We march from Westwood all the way up the hill to UCLA's campus. And then all of us, this huge group of people, stand there, quiet, holding candles, holding hands and swaying like we all hear the same song. Even though it's for a sad reason, it's sort of beautiful.

Then one voice starts singing. Low and quiet. "We shall overcome," she sings, and everyone who knows the words starts singing too. When the song is over, we blow out our candles. And I can tell the protest is over.

My family is pretty solemn on the way home, and it's like no one wants to be first to break the silence, but then Daddy clears his throat.

"How about some ice cream?" he asks.

The only answer to that question is a big fat yes.

I get a double scoop of pistachio, and Hana gets her boring chocolate chip, and Daddy gets cake batter with cookie pieces crumbled in it.

"Lord, you all make my mouth hurt just thinking about all that sugar," Momma says, and then she orders a small mango sherbet.

We sit inside, and it's like we're sitting inside a scoop of ice cream, it smells so sweet.

"You can't let the problems of the world stop you from enjoying life," Daddy says with his mouth full of ice cream.

Momma gives him one of her sweet looks that usually make me and Hana roll our eyeballs right out of our heads, but tonight we let her get away with it.

Then Daddy reaches over and grips Hana's hand. "You and your friends need to be careful out on these streets, you hear me? You can't be giving anybody a reason to hassle you."

"Like they need a reason," Hana says, licking a drip of ice cream off her cone.

"Did you hear what I said?" Daddy's voice has that

serious edge that means you best pay attention.

"Okay," Hana says in a quiet voice.

When we get back home, I write about all the things I observed at the march. When the phone rings, I don't even think about it before picking up. I'm completely ready to stop being angry at my friends.

"Hello?"

"Oh, hey, um, Shayla, this is uh, this is—"

"Hi, Tyler." I cut him off; life is short.

"Oh, yeah, hey. Heh, heh, um, yeah, you recognize my voice, huh?"

"Something like that," I say, starting to bite a hang-nail. "What's up?"

"Yeah, uh, well, I've been hangin' out with my boys, you know. Just um, doing . . . stuff. And, well, I, uh, I've kinda been thinking about you. You know, wondering what you were doing."

"Not much," I say.

Then there's a big pot of nothing, and I wait for Tyler to think of something else to say. I can hear him breathing. One of us has to say something.

"Oh, I went to a march for Black Lives Matter."

"That sounds cool." Tyler sounds relieved that he

has something to say, but I don't want to start talking to Tyler in any type of way.

"Yeah, it was," I say. "Hey, I gotta go."

"Okay, but um, what I wanted to ask you . . . I mean, real quick, I just wanted to know, uh . . ." He pauses for a minute.

I sputter out, "I'll talk to you at school," and hang up. For the rest of vacation I don't answer the phone, and my parents are under strict instructions to say I'm busy if Tyler calls again. (Momma says a boy doesn't have any business calling me anyway.) I don't want to tell my friends about Tyler calling, because that will just lead us back to the dance and that will make me mad all over again.

Daddy asks me very sarcastically, "Is there anyone you *are* talking to?"

I don't even bother answering him.

Silence can be super loud.

40
What's Up?

Being away from school and not having my cell phone, I feel like I've fallen right out of the world. I have no clue what's going on with anybody. I miss all the pictures and videos and updates. Momma won't let me use the computer for any social media. She says the computer is strictly for homework and she doesn't want me distracted, even though I explain I don't have any homework over the holidays. And I try telling her it will be much better for me to watch silly Snapchat videos than to watch the news and see protests getting uglier and uglier. I don't see much peaceful singing anymore. I've seen more and more store windows getting broken, and crowds are getting bigger at the protests. A crowd of people blocked the entrance of a police station and wouldn't move until cops started arresting everyone.

I keep waiting to hear that the trial is over, but I guess it takes a while for arguments to close. And I don't want to believe that officer is going to be found innocent, but I can tell Momma and Daddy are both thinking that's the way it's going to go. Based on the protests happening around the city, that's what a whole bunch of people think too—mostly Black people. "Is someone else going to get killed, Momma?"

Momma turns off the TV. "You don't need to watch any more of that mess," she says.

For the first time, I'm almost glad to go back to school.

Isabella and Julia are by the snack machines at break, waiting for me. I guess they didn't want to risk me not showing up at our spot.

"Hey," I say, as if we just talked yesterday.

Isabella grabs my arm. "Shay! People have been talking about you and Tyler online! Like you two are—"

Before Isabella can finish telling me what people have said about me and Tyler, he appears out of nowhere. Like she called him or something.

"Hey, Shayla, uh, how you doin'?" he asks, looking at the ground.

"I'm good, Tyler." I want to go to our usual spot behind the portables, but I don't know how to get us there. "What's up?" I ask, hoping he'll go away fast.

"Nothing" is all he says, and he doesn't leave.

"Oookay," I say, and angle away from him. "What did you do over vacation?" I ask Isabella and Julia, making it clear that's who I'm talking to. "How was art camp, Is?"

"Fine," Isabella answers, looking at Tyler. "Fun, I mean. And I spent time with my dad." She coughs a few times. "He was sick, though."

Isabella must've caught whatever her dad had, because she looks awful. Instead of her usual bronzy color, she's almost the color of mustard.

"Obachan asked about you. She made the kushiyaki you like," Julia says accusingly.

Going to Julia's grandmother's is one of my favorite things—especially if she's cooking. She usually tells me how she's going to fatten me up. "I'm . . . sorry I missed it," I say in a low voice. I bet I missed a lot of things. I give a side glance at Tyler and then look away fast.

"Shayla went to a rally for Black Lives Matter," he says.

Julia and Isabella both look wide-eyed at me.

"Yeah," I say. My palms itch as if fire ants are biting them all over. I need Tyler to leave so I can find out what people are saying about us.

"How do you know what Shayla did?" Julia asks him.

"She told me," Tyler says, like duh. "Over break. We were, uh, talking."

My cheeks are so hot, my skin might start melting off my face.

"You were?" Isabella asks, looking back and forth between me and Tyler.

"He called me," I say, as if he's not standing right there.

"And you talked to *him*," Julia says, and raises an eyebrow.

I don't know what to say. Luckily, the bell rings, saving me from having to say anything.

Isabella runs off to class, but Julia waits like she wants to see what me and Tyler are going to do.

"Bye," I say, and start to walk away, but Tyler walks next to me.

Julia turns on her heel and walks off fast. She doesn't even say goodbye.

"You have PE next, right?" Tyler asks, trying to keep up with me.

I walk faster. "How do you know?"

"Me too. I just have a different teacher. But I've seen you." His face breaks out into an embarrassed grin.

There's four other PE classes going at the same time as mine, and I've never noticed Tyler. Of course, I've never been looking for him.

We get to the locker room at the same time as Yolanda. We're both a little out of breath.

"Hey," Yolanda says.

I wish I could tell her it's no big deal. I wish I could tell her something so she'd stop looking at me like I have a mushroom growing out of my forehead.

"See you later, Tyler," I say firmly, to stop him from following me into the girls' locker room.

When Yolanda and I get outside for roll call, she seems like she's in a bad mood. Coach West has us all partner up and start doing sit-ups.

Yolanda holds my feet while I struggle to do fifty sit-ups. "What's going on with you and Tyler?" she blurts out at sit-up twenty-two.

I sit up. I shrug. I go back down. I don't want to tell

Yolanda anything until I talk to my friends.

"But you don't even like him," Yolanda says, raising her voice a little.

Up again. "It's not . . . I just . . ." I look at Yolanda and shrug at her crown of braids. She gives my feet a hard squeeze. I go back down.

"I don't get why a boy would like a girl who's mean to him," she says.

"Haven't you noticed me being nicer?" I feel like I have a big shovel in my hand and am just digging myself into a deeper and deeper hole.

"No," Yolanda says, letting go of my feet even though I've only done forty sit-ups.

I have no clue why she seems mad at me. She was the one who wanted me to be nice to Tyler.

41
Later

In English, Ms. Jacobs reminds us again to keep up with our eyeball journals. "There's a lot going on right now," she says. "Quite a lot to observe and *think* about. Remember, make your *own* minds up."

She's staring right at me.

Then she claps her hands and starts talking about prepositional phrases.

After class, I run into Isabella in the hallway, which is weird because her fourth period isn't on this floor.

But here she is, right in the middle of the swarm of people, with her hands on her hips, letting everyone bump into us.

"Why were you avoiding me and Julia all winter break? Are you mad at us? Are you mad at *me*?"

I squish us out of the middle of the hall, off to the side. Someone's backpack whacks me in the shoulder.

For the first time, I'm glad there's so many people because it takes a minute to wade through everyone, which is good because I need a minute to figure out what I want to say.

I really want Jace to like me. And I really, really want him to *not* like Isabella. But I also want my friends back. I think about Coach West's story. I press against the wall of lockers and catch my breath. "We're good." I smile to try and show her how good we are. "I wasn't avoiding you guys. I was grounded. I don't have my phone." I feel like I'm playing that game Two Truths and a Lie. I bet Isabella can figure out which part of what I said isn't true.

"But you've been talking to *Tyler*?" Her voice sounds raspy.

"No! Well, yeah, he called me, but we haven't been *talking*." I know I sound ridiculous. "What have people been saying?"

"I'll tell you when you tell me what's really going on," Isabella says. I can tell she's frustrated with me, because her eyebrows are so close together, it's almost like her unibrow is back.

I feel frustrated too. It is totally unfair that I'm stuck with two boys liking me who I don't like at *all*, while she gets the one I do like. And explaining about Tyler is too complicated. I really need to know what people are saying. "Come on, Is, please," I beg. "Just tell me."

Isabella puts her hands on her hips. *"No,"* she says. "You first."

My eyes open really wide at that. I don't know if I've ever heard Isabella say no like that. I'm so shocked, I almost tell her right there, but I still don't know exactly *what* to say. "I'll tell you later, okay? Let's go eat lunch."

"Fine," Isabella says, and we walk to the overhang area without saying anything else.

Before Isabella and I can sit down, Julia walks up . . . with Tyler.

"Hey, Shayla, look who I bumped into," Julia says. "He was looking for you." She says it like this is fine and totally normal.

It's *not* fine, and no way is it normal. Why can't Tyler leave me alone? And why did Julia have to bring him to our lunch table?

"Hey, Shayla," Tyler says softly.

We all just stand there for a second; I feel like my friends are waiting to see what I'm going to do. I hate how it feels between us now, like we are china plates trying not to get cracked.

I sit down and open my lunch. "I'm starved," I say, just as if there isn't some sweaty boy staring at me. I don't know what else to do.

Isabella and Julia sit too, but Tyler just stands there.

"Um, go ahead and sit down, Tyler," Isabella says.

Tyler sits down right away, and of course he sits right next to me.

Isabella watches me like I'm a science experiment, and Julia looks back and forth between me and Tyler like she's at the movies. I bet she wishes she had some popcorn.

I manage to get through the whole lunch period without ever speaking to Tyler directly. It isn't even that hard.

When the bell rings, some of Tyler's friends walk by and see him sitting next to me. They start smiling and laughing and throwing punches at each other. Sometimes I really hate boys. He gets up and runs off with them. Well, first he puts his hand on my shoulder, and *then* he runs off. His hand is hot and sweaty, and I feel like he has left a big Tyler print on me.

As we're throwing our trash away, Isabella says, "Is it *later* yet?"

"I have to get to class," I say.

42
As If

Tyler shows all of his little teeth at me in shop. "Hey," he says.

"Hey," I say back.

"You, uh, want me to, like, help you, you know, get started on your birdhouse?" He looks hopefully at the pieces of wood I have in my hand.

"Thanks, I got it," I say.

Yolanda smiles at Tyler like he is one of her little brothers or something. "You can help me, Ty."

"Yeah, okay then," he says.

After class he puts his hand on my arm and leans forward like he is—oh no! I jerk away. He might've tricked me into one kiss, but there is no way he is getting another one!

"See you later," I say.

I can't get out of class fast enough.

But it's like I can't escape Tyler even when he's not around.

At practice, Angie and Natalie break away from relay team practice and come up to me. Angie says, "You and Ty need to hang with us at lunch sometimes."

I gulp down the thoughts that are super close to spilling out of my mouth. Like, why is Angie asking me to sit with her at lunch now? She doesn't think I'm suddenly cool just because of *Tyler*, does she? "That'd be fun," I say, meaning *me* hanging with them would be fun. Not me and *Ty*.

"I'll save you a spot," Angie says.

I will not be sitting at the basketball courts anytime soon. I'm trying to figure out how to lose sweaty boy, not be more connected to him. "Um," I say, digging the toe of my shoe into the track.

"You better be careful, though. Steph said if you break Tyler's heart, she's coming after you," Natalie says, frowning at me. Natalie has never been nice to me, and it doesn't look like she's about to start.

"Steph?"

"Tyler's cousin? Stephanie?"

I didn't even know Tyler *had* a cousin at Emerson.

"Yeah, you take care of Ty," Angie warns.

"Tyler's nice, um," I start. "I don't really . . ." I start again. What am I going to say? What am I going to do?

Oh my god! Everyone thinks me and Tyler are talking!! AS IF!!!!!!!!

I have a bad feeling about this whole thing, and it is Julia's fault! I wasn't even playing Command—this is so totally unfair!

Why did I ever let him kiss me???????

43
Blocks

For some track events you use blocks. They're these foot brace things that sit on the track and let you be in a ready position to start charging down your lane. Using blocks looks like it should be easy. You just put your feet on, wait for the starting pistol, and push off, right? *Not* right. You're hunched over with your butt sticking up, your feet pressed hard against the pedals, your itchy palms raised, with just the tips of your fingers on the gritty track, waiting. And when the starting pistol sounds, you push off and go! Except. It's not easy to push yourself out hard enough to get you going, but not so hard that you fall flat on your face. And sometimes you just get stuck in the blocks. You aren't really "stuck," but it sure feels as if there are hands gripping your feet, and not letting you go.

I was hoping Tyler hanging around was just a one-day thing, but he shows up again before my friends and I can get to our spot behind the portables, and the four of us stand there awkwardly. It sure feels like I am stuck in the blocks. I work so hard to get my voice to say something. But I don't actually know what to say. Julia and Isabella start talking to each other, and I watch them as if I don't know who they are. Isabella throws a few rabbity looks my way, but then it's like she gives up. She makes Julia crack up over a story about her little brother eating doughnuts, but I feel like I can't laugh. She wasn't really talking to me. Tyler is talking to me. And talking and talking.

When the bell rings, Tyler walks me to PE just like he did yesterday, but this time we don't see Yolanda, and when I do see her in class with her mass of curls on either side of her head, she acts super sour and I don't know at all what to do about it.

And then lunch rolls around.

I grab my lunch from my locker but can't muster up my standard slam, and then I make my way outside. Isabella and Julia are both waiting for me. They each grab one of my arms and start running. It's like a kidnapping! I don't know where we're going, but I know what's going on. We are ditching Tyler.

We giggle all the way to our spot behind the portables. It's almost empty here at lunch. There's no tables or anything, so it's harder to eat, but it's private.

As soon as we get settled, though, all the giggling stops, and Isabella has a coughing fit. She points at Julia, like, *You go first.*

"Okay, so, yo, why are you acting so awful?" Julia asks. Her lips are tight and she has one eyebrow raised.

"Yeah," Isabella says, and her voice sounds really hoarse now.

I look back and forth between my friends. "What? I'm not."

Julia says, "You didn't talk to us all winter break, and there is a thing called a landline, you know."

"We were calling you and you never would come to the phone," Isabella says, and folds her arms tight across her chest. I don't know if it's because she's mad or if she's trying to hold her coughs back.

"Yeah," Julia says, getting loud. "Obviously, there's something going on with you and Tyler, and we don't know what it is." She clenches her hands on her hips, waiting for me to say something.

I hate that Julia and Isabella made me feel like we

were having a fun secret adventure, when really they just wanted to yell at me. "Well, you two weren't being good friends to me," I say. "You set me up, Julia, and then you told Isabella she should go for Jace!"

They both just stare at me for a second, and then Julia explodes. "You read our texts?" She sounds shocked, and like *I'm* the one who did the worse thing.

I don't bother denying it. "That's not the point. You shouldn't have told her that."

Julia says, "If Jace likes Isabella, you should let her have him. A good friend wouldn't stand in the way."

"But—" Isabella starts.

"I don't know how you can say what a good friend would do, Julia. It's not like you're such a good friend anymore!" I yell.

"Just because of a dumb command?" Julia asks. "I said I was sorry. And I don't think you should be mad at us that Jace isn't into you. We should be mad at you for being a Snoopy McSnoop-face."

"Fine!" I shout, not even caring that people are around. "I shouldn't have read the messages. But you're always with your *squad*, like Isabella and I don't even count."

"High key, much?" Julia says to me. "Jeez! So sometimes I sit with my squad and sometimes with you. You don't have to be all salty about it. I've been friends with most of them for a long time too."

"And you talk like Stacy now," I say.

"Yo, are you for real?" Julia sounds shocked, like she doesn't know what I'm talking about. "You have zero chill, Shayla." She blows her hair out of her eyes in a big exasperated puff.

Before I can show Julia just how little chill I have, Isabella says, "It *has* been weird, Jules." Her voice isn't angry like mine would've been; she just sounds serious. "It used to be just us. You know, the United Nations. And you didn't talk like that before."

"Things *change*," Julia says, and sighs really loud. "And *everybody* talks like that."

"No, *everyone* doesn't," I say. "And we haven't changed. Just you have," I say, not even trying at all to keep the anger out of my voice. Julia can act like she hasn't done anything wrong, but Isabella and I know the truth.

"We're in junior high now! Did you really think we were never going to change?" Julia is close to shouting.

Yes, I want to shout back at her. Is it really that awful to want friendships to stay the same? And to want your friends to back off from the boy you're crushing on? "Stop shouting," I say. "And *fine*. No, I didn't think that. Of course we're going to change, but not like this."

"Can you guys chill out?" Isabella asks. "This isn't—" Whatever she was going to say gets buried in a batch of coughing.

Julia's face gets pinchier. "If it was such a problem with me hanging out with my other friends, why didn't you just say something?" Before Is or I can answer, Julia keeps going. "And, second, we're *older* now. You can't be a baby about stuff." Julia's lips are so tight, they almost disappear. Her voice is super tight too. "If Jace likes Isabella, you should be happy for her."

"But, I don't—" Isabella starts.

"I'm not being a baby!" I shout, not letting Isabella finish. "How am I supposed to be happy about the boy I like liking one of my best friends? It's not *fair*." I'm breathing hard and starting to sweat. I want to grab Julia's shoulders and shake her.

"Well, it's not Isabella's fault," Julia yells.

The few people around are staring at us. "Stop

shouting at me!" I feel like crying and throwing something at the same time.

"Could you two stop talking like I'm not even here?" Isabella shouts.

Her voice is so loud, it makes me jump. I've never heard her sound so mad. "What's the matter with you?" I ask.

Isabella clenches her hands into fists. "You're both acting like my feelings don't matter. Don't speak for me." Talking that loud must hurt, because she grips her throat and her eyes water.

"You know what?" Julia says. "This convo is totally ratchet."

"That's not even how you use the word," I say before I can stop myself.

"I'm out," Julia says. My eyes go extra wide because I can't believe she is just going to walk away and leave this big pot of bad feelings behind. "Jules!" I try to grab her arm, but she moves out of reach.

"Late," she says.

"Fine," I say. I want to ask her who's acting like a baby now.

Isabella and I watch Julia walk away.

Isabella blows hair out of her face, and then she turns to me. "What's the matter with you two?"

"Nothing's wrong with *me*," I say.

"That whole thing was dumb," she says. "I don't even *like* Jace. He's cute but he's not very nice. If I was going to like somebody, it wouldn't be him."

I don't like the sound of that. It's almost like Isabella is saying it's dumb to like Jace. "Thanks," I say.

"But I don't even *want* a boyfriend or to be talking to anyone. And that's not even the point," Isabella goes on in her croaky voice. "Even if I *did* like him, I wouldn't have talked to him. That would've been messed up. But you and Julia wouldn't even let me say anything." Her voice gets a little louder with each sentence, and it makes her cough more.

I frown. I don't want one of my friends liking the same boy I like. Why can't I have dibs on a guy I like, whether he likes me or not? But I'm not sure what a friendship manual would say about that. Maybe Julia is right. A good friend wouldn't stand in her friend's way. "I shouldn't have acted so weird," I finally say. "Guess it's not your fault you're scorching."

"No, you shouldn't have," Isabella says, ignoring the

compliment. "Because you know what's really messed up? That you didn't already know I wouldn't do that to you. You should've known better." With her looking so sick, she looks really sorrowful, but her voice sounds strong.

I've never heard her sound so forceful. And even though she's spilling her new force all over me, she sounds good. Raspy, but good. "You're right."

She gets a napkin out of her lunch bag and blows her nose. "So don't do that again, okay?"

"Okay. Check. Got it. One hundred."

We fist-bump that business. Then Isabella says, "She was right, you know. We should've said something. Told Julia we missed it being the three of us."

"I guess," I say. I'm not sure if I agree. It seems like Julia should've known without us having to say anything.

Isabella sighs, then pulls her hair to the side and starts braiding it. "I'm so hot," she says, but she shivers and pulls her sweater tight around her. Then she gives me a stern look. "Okay, so tell me. Why *have* you been letting Tyler hang around?"

I stare at the tiny pearl buttons on Isabella's sweater.

"It started at the dance, because Bernard was . . . acting like maybe he liked me? I thought he'd leave me alone if he thought I was interested in someone else." It feels good to finally talk about it.

Isabella wipes sweat off her forehead. "You could've just told him you weren't interested. Like, thanks, but no thanks?"

"I was scared. Bernard still freaks me out. He can be okay sometimes, but if he doesn't get what he wants, he gets all shouty and mad. I didn't want him to yell at me."

Isabella starts coughing, so it takes a few seconds before she can talk, but then she says, "I guess I can understand why you sort of pretended so that Bernard would back off, but you can't have everyone at school thinking you and Tyler are, like, *talking*."

"Why not? He doesn't really bug me all that much. I just ignore him. He seems happy," I say.

"But it's mean," she says sternly.

"Mean?" I have no clue what she is talking about.

"Yes!" Isabella smashes her lunch bag into a clump. "How would you feel if a guy was letting you hang around like a puppy dog?"

I hadn't thought about it that way. "I think it would

be meaner if I told him I didn't like him."

"Don't tell him *that*! But figure something out," Isabella says, using her new forceful voice.

"Ugh," I say, because I know she's right but I sure don't want to have to deal with Tyler.

Isabella laughs but then starts coughing so hard, I'm ready to catch one of her lungs.

I offer her some water but she waves it away. Once she catches her breath, I ask her, "So what are we going to do about Julia?"

Isabella shrugs. She looks sad, and I bet I look the same way. "I don't know. But walking off like that sure doesn't solve anything." She sniffs loudly. "Ugh, this cold is killing me."

Then the bell rings and we head to fifth period.

All through math I wonder if the United Nations is permanently divided.

I wonder how Julia could just walk away.

I wonder how I'm going to break up with someone who's not really my boyfriend.

I haven't figured anything out by the time I get to shop, so I just stay bent over my birdhouse and ignore Tyler. He gets close to me a few times, but maybe he can

237

feel me thinking *Go away* at him because he backs off. I can hear him and Yolanda joking around, and I'm glad she doesn't try to pull me into their conversation. I've never been so happy for shop to be over, and I zoom out of class without even telling Yolanda goodbye.

Maybe I'll be able to figure out this Tyler mess at track practice.

Today we're practicing our starts out of the blocks.

"Try focusing on the first hurdle," Coach West says. "Don't think so much about getting out of the blocks."

I bend lower and keep my fingers pressed against the track. I can hear my breathing. It sounds shaky. All the hurdles stretch in front of me like a big row of problems.

The first hurdle is figuring out what to say to Tyler. The second is deciding when to tell him. The third is wondering if I should call Julia when I get home.

Coach West puts her hand on my back. "Calm down, Shayla. You just need to be patient and focus. Block everything out and just wait for the starter pistol."

"I'm trying," I say.

Bernard walks by, tossing his shot up and down, and shouts, "Looking good, Shay!" at me.

I almost fall right on my face. He really needs to work on his volume control.

Coach West backs away a little. "Concentrate, Shayla."

The relay girls are standing on the side of the track, having a water break. They're nudging each other, looking at me, and laughing. If I were them, I'd be laughing too. Despite what Bernard said, I know I look ridiculous with my bottom stuck up in the air.

When Coach West notices me staring at them, she claps her hands at me. "You're focusing on the wrong thing."

I nod and stare down the track at the hurdle. My stomach hurts and I feel like the blocks are yanking on my feet, holding me back.

44
The Breaks

The next day, when I go outside for break, I'm looking for Isabella. But instead I see Tyler.

And I'm alone with him.

I hate not having my cell phone. Isabella would've texted me to tell me she'd be out sick, and I could've been prepared. Or I could've texted Julia and begged her to hang out with me even if we're both still angry. That would have been easy with a text. I don't think I could've said it out loud.

This is why cell phones are so important.

I've never been in a fight with one of my best friends before. I'm not even sure if we are in a fight.

Tyler is smiling and stuttering at me and asking me if I know about some video game. (I don't.) It is the perfect time to tell him he got it all wrong about us, but I can't figure out how to say it that won't sound awful. Especially since I'm mad at him. I know I shouldn't have let this whole talking thing go on, but he shouldn't have kissed me like that. Everybody knows you don't put your chapped lips all over somebody without permission. At least they *should* know.

Tyler starts talking about the trial and how messed up it will be if the jury gets it wrong, and even though I agree with him, I don't tell him that. I tap my foot impatiently, and instead of saying anything I want to, I do a bunch of nodding. And then the bell rings, so I'm saved from having to say anything.

But lunch is just a couple of hours away.

I don't even have that long.

Tyler ambushes me in between third and fourth period. He pulls me over to a corner in the hallway, and I'm caught.

"Hey, Tyler, can we talk later? I have to get to class." I'm not even lying. No way do I want Ms. Jacobs mad at me for being late.

"Yeah, okay, but I need to ask you something first." He takes a deep breath and then blurts out, "Are you my girl?"

"Tyler." I clear my throat. "I think you have the wrong idea about us."

He is quiet for a minute; I watch a small muscle in his cheek bunch up and then he just stares at me.

I sigh loud enough for him to hear. "Tyler, why do you even like me?"

He smiles a real quick shy smile, and then he looks down at his shoes. "'Cause, you know. You're cute and all."

"Thanks," I say. I feel worse. I wasn't trying to get a compliment out of him. My cheeks feel like they're steaming, they are so hot. I swallow. "But you can't like somebody just because of the way they look. Maybe you should, you know, like somebody who's nice to you and likes you back?"

Hearing myself say that out loud stings. All I've cared about with Jace is how he looks. He's never acted as if he likes me, and I haven't paid a bit of attention to that.

Tyler smiles at me, but then he stops smiling. I think what I said just hit him. His eyebrows get close together and he leans forward. I take a small step back. I'm never going to let someone kiss me again unless I want them to.

"Uh, okay, it's all good." He pauses, and I'm just about to try and walk away, but then he keeps going. "It's just, like, at the dance—"

"That was a command. And I didn't even kiss you back."

"Seemed like it to me."

"Well, I didn't! And you should know it's not cool to just kiss somebody. You can't be all up on somebody who didn't say it was okay. Not even if it's a command!" I don't think I knew how much it bothered me until I hear myself telling him off. I don't care anymore who hears us. That kiss was awful, and even if I had been playing Command too, Tyler shouldn't have done it.

I can tell he knows I'm right by the guilty look on his face. "You need permission and I never said yes."

"I'm sorry," he says, and his shoulders slump. "Coach West told me the same thing."

"Good," I say. Then I add, "Don't do it again," and Tyler nods.

I think we're done, but Tyler dips his head down a little, clears his throat, and then looks back up, staring me right in the eyes.

"So why you been lettin' me hang around and all?"

243

He asks so quietly, I almost can't hear him.

I have no answer. I can't meet his eyes and stare instead at his chin. I twist the end of my ponytail round and round. When I don't say anything, he just nods, like he understands.

"I guess I'll see you around, then," he says, and turns away, dipping into the crowd filing by on their way to class. I see Natalie, and she frowns at me.

I figure word will get around that Tyler and I "broke up."

Maybe if Julia hears about it, she'll sit with me at lunch.

45
Not So Great

She doesn't. If Julia knows Isabella is out sick today, she knows that means I don't have anyone to sit with. But she doesn't come look for me. She isn't at our table. I don't even see her at lunch.

I feel totally lost. The great thing about a three-way friendship is if someone is absent, you still have a friend to sit with at lunch. I can't sit at a table all by myself.

I consider wandering over to the basketball courts, but that would be a bad plan. Tyler would be over there. Besides, it's probably not the best reason to go over to the courts now just because my other friends aren't around.

I could go to the library. Some people sit in there for lunch, but it's sort of where you sit if you don't have friends.

I end up sitting on a bench by the office. I made the

mistake of putting tomatoes on my sandwich, and they made the bread all soggy. Even my sandwich is sad. And then a shadow blocks out the sun.

"What are you doin' over here by yourself?"

I look up at Jace and my mouth opens, but no words come out.

"You all right?"

I shut my mouth and swallow the soggy lump of sandwich. And then I nod at him.

Jace smiles at me.

Jace smiles at me.

Jace smiles at me.

"So what's going on?" he asks. He has one of those spinny things and spins it and lets it go round and round on the top of his finger.

"Nothing much," I say, trying to sound like him talking to me is at the very bottom of things I care about. "Pretty chill, you know. Very low key." I should totally shut up.

"So where's your friend?" Jace asks.

I'm so wrapped up in the moment of him actually talking to me that at first I think he's asking about Julia, because I had wondered the same thing. And then my brain goes, *Well, that's silly—he doesn't even know Julia,* so I think, *Oh, he must mean Tyler.* But then, it registers. Hard.

"Oh, she's sick," I say flatly, feeling a little sick myself.

"Oh, yeah?" he says.

Then he surprises me by sitting down. Right next to me, which makes me feel like I'm going to swallow my tongue or something. I tell myself, *Okay, breathe, yeah, he asked about Isabella, but he's sitting right here next to you.* He's sitting close enough for our arms to touch.

And then he asks, "Is she talking to anybody?"

"Who?" I ask, not quite able to keep myself from staring at him.

"Who we talkin' about, girl?" Jace asks, like I'm stupid.

"Oh, Is? I mean Isabella?" I laugh. *Ha, ha! This is so very, very funny.* "She's not, I mean, she's sort of . . ." I sound completely stupid. "Uh, I mean, she, um, she uh, is, uh . . ." I want to tell him about Isabella's mom not allowing her to have a boyfriend or something, but my mouth won't let me say it. "She isn't talking to anybody right now," I admit.

Jace smiles big and leans against the wall. I know that smile. I have seen it on Hana's face a million times. It is the smile that says, *I can have whatever I want, because I am all that.* And I know it's true.

I think he'll leave then, but he just keeps sitting with me. I actually wish he would leave. He is making my palms itch and my stomach hurt.

He starts talking about hating history and how he has a bad grade and how it's all Mr. Powell's fault.

"Do you do your homework?" I ask.

Jace scowls at me. "I do enough. He's just a punk and he wears those dumb scarves like what my mama would wear."

"What?" I say. "Mr. Powell's the best." I move over so our arms can't touch anymore.

Jace gives me a what's-with-you look, but I don't care. I think about him talking about my forehead. And being mean to Alex. I try to think of one time I saw him being nice, but I can't think of any.

I sat next to Jace today.

It wasn't so great.

248

46
Dog Pile

I'm on my way to fifth period when I realize that the girls behind me, who are talking really loud, are actually talking about *me*.

"Makes me sick, the way she thinks she's all that."

"I guess she's just too good for your cousin."

"Somebody needs to teach her a lesson."

The school handbook has a whole section on harassment and how we aren't supposed to do it. But I'm almost positive I'm being harassed. I have heard about dog-piling, where a bunch of people jump on you. It sounds horrible. Am I going to get dog-piled? My stomach knots up with fear, and I run into the girls' bathroom.

This is a pretty stupid decision, because they just follow right behind me.

I whirl around to ask them why are they messing

with me, but when I see Angie, my mouth just drops open like I'm in the doctor's office and he wants me to say *ahhhhhh*. I'm not surprised at all to see Natalie. With them is a big girl who I found out recently is Stephanie, Tyler's cousin.

"Yo, you think you're too good for Ty?" Stephanie has small mean eyes. She snaps her fingers at me.

"No, I don't," I say, taking a small step back. "Why don't you leave me alone?"

"Leave me alone," Natalie says in a whiny, fakey voice, as if that's how I sounded.

I for sure don't want to get dog-piled or just generally messed with. I look at the door, but I would have to get through them to get to it. I try to remember everything Hana has told me about fighting. She's really good at it.

"You know what? I think it's time this Oreo found out she's not as cute as she thinks she is," Natalie says.

Oreo? Seriously? I'm not white on the inside, Black on the outside. "What's your issue?" I ask.

Stephanie is starting to get close to me like she wants to grab at me or something. "You broke my cousin's heart," she says.

Uh, dramatic much? "I didn't," I say. "I like Tyler." Obviously I don't mean *like* like, but I don't want Stephanie thinking I was mean to him. Because I wasn't. Was I?

"Yeah, right," Natalie says. "Why'd you break up with him, then?"

"We weren't even talking or, you know, boyfriend and girlfriend. He kissed me because of that stupid Command game. And he knows that wasn't cool. If he wanted to kiss me, he needed to ask. I don't know why you all thought we were together."

"Who's 'you all'?" Angie asks, making little quotation marks in the air. I didn't know Angie could sound so mean. "Are you talking about *A-fri-can A-mer-i-cans*?" She stretches the words really long, like I have a hard time understanding English or something. "Well, I hate to tell you this, but *you all* is you too."

"I know that!" I can't believe Angie is going there. "'You all,' as in *everybody*!"

"No one can figure you out," Stephanie says. "You tried to act all down and then you dogged my cousin."

"I'm sorry if I hurt Tyler's feelings." I say. "But it's not my fault I didn't like him like that."

"You don't like him because he's Black!" Natalie says like I walked into some kind of trap.

"Oh yeah? Then why do I like Jace?"

Angie's and Natalie's eyes both go so wide, it's like a flash popped in their faces.

47
Wanna Go?

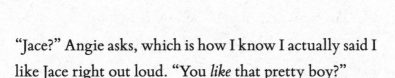

"Jace?" Angie asks, which is how I know I actually said I like Jace right out loud. "You *like* that pretty boy?"

I want to say that I actually don't think I like Jace all that much anymore, but this doesn't seem like the right time.

"Okay," Angie says, "if you're so *down*, how come you don't hang out with anybody?"

(Translation: *anybody* = Black kids.) "I just hang with my friends from elementary school. We've been friends a long time."

"Yeah, I heard you didn't have any Black friends in elementary either," Stephanie says.

"There weren't that many of us in the same grade," I mutter. Which is totally true. There was me, Berika, Tonja, Alonzo, and Bernard.

"Yeah, and you were too good for them, huh?" Stephanie asked.

Had Berika or Tonja said that about me? Is that what they thought? "I was *not*!"

"Then why don't you sit with us at lunch?" Natalie asks.

"Because I sit with my *friends*," I say. It sure seems like I'm repeating myself. Why is it so hard for people to understand that I'm not doing anything wrong by hanging out with my best friends?

"I bet you don't have a single Black friend," Stephanie says.

I start to say I'm friends with Yolanda, but I'm not sure if I can truly claim her. I'm not sure what she'd say if they asked her. She has been acting weird ever since the Tyler thing.

It seemed like Angie and I were sort of friends, but obviously that's not true.

"Thinking you're all that with your big ol' forehead," Stephanie says.

That is the wrong thing to say to me.

I tighten my hands into fists. "Fine." I say. "You wanna go? Come on, then."

48
Fight!

I will fight all three of them.

All together or one at a time. I sort of wish I had some earrings to take off. Hana told me that's when you know a girl is seriously ready to fight.

Then Angie does the one thing I sure don't expect.

She starts giggling.

Stephanie takes a step away from Angie. "What's wrong with you?"

That makes Angie's giggles turn to full-on laughter.

"What's so funny?" Natalie asks.

"Yeah, what?" I ask. I do not see one thing funny in this whole situation.

Angie takes a deep breath and tries to stop laughing. "Well, she did say *us*, didn't she, when she was talking about the Black kids at her school?"

I don't relax my fists; I'm still ready to fight if I have to.

"I do believe she's ready to throw down, Steph." For some reason, Angie finds this to be hilarious. "Now *that's* a Black girl for you," she says, laughing so hard, I think she might hyperventilate.

I know it's not true that all Black girls want to fight, but Angie thinking I was ready to, and me imagining myself taking on three girls at once, makes my hands relax and gets me laughing too, and the next thing I know, Natalie is almost smiling. Stephanie is not.

"Come on y'all, let's get to class. We're already late," Angie says.

As we leave the bathroom, we run right into Coach West.

"Don't you girls need to be in class?" she asks, looking at all of us suspiciously. I think she looks at me especially hard.

"Yes, Coach!" we yell, and rush off.

In shop, I try and joke around with Yolanda, but she is in a bad mood or something and stays bent over her project. I ignore the looks Tyler keeps sending my way. I want to tell him I'm sorry, but I'm not sure what I'd be apologizing for. Should I be *sorry* for not liking him?

And if that's true, shouldn't there be a bunch of guys—starting with Jace—apologizing to *me*? Besides, Tyler was the one who was wrong for kissing me in the first place.

When the bell rings, I don't rush outside. Coach West called an extra practice, saying we've gotten soft over winter break, and I'm dreading it. I might've been ready to fight a little bit ago, but I'm sure not anymore. I hope none of the other girls wants to.

49
No Justice, No Peace

Nobody is trying to fight me, but track is still sort of awful. Even though we ended up laughing over the ridiculousness of me trying to fight them, I guess Natalie and Angie aren't exactly cool with me yet.

All four relay team girls ignore me, and I wonder if Carmetta and Maya think I dogged Tyler too.

Angie comes into the lane two over from me to practice hurdling, and I catch her eyes and try and send her a whole lot of words in that one look. How I want to be friends, and it's a joke to say I think I'm too good when I don't think I'm very good at all, and that we are both sisters so we're connected, and that it was silly for me to act like Tyler and I were talking, but I didn't mean anything mean by it.

Maybe a fraction of what I was trying to say, Angie

caught, because she does give me a half smile. But then she just goes past me in a blur.

Practice starts to wind down, and we're all stretching out our sore muscles and guzzling water.

Coach West's phone has been rattling on a bench for the last few minutes, but she's been ignoring it. But when it starts vibrating again, she picks it up and reads something. I'm guessing it's bad news, because her face gets worried and sort of sad. She sighs and then blows her whistle a few times. "Let's wrap it up! Clean up and clear out."

I want to ask her if everything is okay, but she crosses her arms tight and stares up at the clouds and I can hear the words *don't bother me*, even though she doesn't say a word.

We all help to put away the practice equipment and move the hurdles off the track, and then we head out to the front of the school to wait for our rides.

When I climb into the car, I notice Momma's expression right away. She looks a whole lot like the way Coach West was looking when she got that message on her phone.

"What's wrong?" I ask Momma. My stomach

squeezes, like I drank way too much water.

Momma doesn't answer right away. She has her bottom lip clenched by her teeth, but then finally she lets go of the sigh she's been holding. "Verdict came back. They found that police officer not guilty."

"What?" I say, not because I didn't hear her, but because there's no way what she said could be true. "But there was a video!"

"I know, Shayla." Momma almost sounds like she's mad at me.

"How could that happen?" I ask. "She shot that man."

"The jury must've believed she thought her life was in jeopardy."

"But he was walking *away*." As much as I hated seeing that video, I've watched a bunch of times. All I saw was a man walking slowly to his truck. And then a police officer start shooting. Shooting until the man fell down in the street.

"I *know*, Shayla."

That's when I notice a tear slowly working its way down Momma's cheek. One lonely, sad tear that slides down to her chin, and then Momma swipes it away with the back of her hand.

Seeing Momma cry makes me want to cry too. My chest gets heavy and my throat gets so small, it's hard to swallow. My eyes start to burn, and even though the tears don't come, it feels like I've been crying for days.

On the drive home, we pass a big group of people standing at an intersection, waving signs and shouting. They're shouting so loud, I can hear them even though my window is rolled up. They're shouting about how we matter. How we need justice. How the verdict was racist.

I see a sign that says *Honk for Justice!* and so I tell Momma to honk her horn, but she doesn't.

When we get home, Hana and Daddy are talking in the family room. It looks like Hana's been crying.

Hana never cries. Even when she gets checked real hard in a game.

Daddy looks up at Momma. "You heard?"

"People already out protesting." Momma goes and sits next to Daddy. I stand there, wanting to curl up in Momma's lap but knowing I'm too old for that.

I don't know what to do.

A car horn beeps outside, and Hana wipes her face with a quick brush of her hand and jumps off the couch. "That's Regina," she says, and heads to the front door.

"Hana," Daddy says, and I'm sure he's going to tell her she can't go, that it might be unsafe out there, that she needs to stay right here at home, but all he says is "Be careful. Don't do anything stupid."

"Momma?" I say, hoping Momma will stop my sister. Outside seems scary and unsafe.

She holds her hand out to me, and I join her on the couch. "You heard your father?" she asks Hana.

"I'll be okay," Hana says, and then she's gone.

50
The 405

"Where did Hana go?" I ask Momma.

Momma has a rule about us all eating as a family. Nothing is supposed to get in the way of the four of us all sitting down at the same time. When it's basketball season and Hana has practice, we have to eat either super early or super late. But Hana's not back yet, and Momma is spooning out the red beans and rice.

"Momma?"

She looks over at Daddy, and he looks back at her.

And then Daddy says, "Your sister is marching on the 405."

"The 405? She's marching on the *freeway*?"

Momma sets the pot down and settles in her chair. She holds out both her hands.

"Why is Hana on the freeway? Did Regina's car

break down? Shouldn't we go and get them?" I ask, taking hold of Momma's hand. Daddy takes my other hand. He has to reach far over because normally he holds Hana's and then she holds mine.

Momma gives my hand a squeeze, and I bow my head.

Usually our prayer before dinner is really fast. Just a quick thank-you to God for the food, and sometimes Daddy will add something silly like thanking God for Momma's brown eyes, or for not getting caught in a traffic jam on the way home from work. But tonight Momma's voice is slow and serious, and after she gives thanks for the food, she says something that makes my eyes pop open.

"And protect our daughter, Hana, as she struggles to understand the horrible shootings and this troubling verdict. Keep her on the path of peace and nonviolence. And give solace to the poor families, Lord, who have lost young men way too soon." Momma gives my hand another squeeze, reminding me I'm supposed to have my eyes closed. I shut them quick. "May we find strength in your love, Lord."

"Amen," we all say together.

"Is . . . is Hana okay?" I ask.

"Yes, sugar," Momma says. "Black Lives Matter organized a march on the 405 to protest the ruling. To make people see that we need to get justice too. You know in this city anything that affects traffic is going to get noticed."

Before I have time to be scared, I ask, "Can I go?"

Momma shakes her head, but Daddy says, "Maybe she should."

"No," Momma says. "I'm not having my baby caught up in that. Not yet."

Sometimes I like it when Momma calls me her baby, and sometimes, like right now, it makes me feel like I'm about two. "But Momma, this is about reminding people that Black lives matter. I'm Black too. I should be supporting us."

"You don't have to march across a freeway to support African Americans. Besides, it's a school night."

I know my mouth has some food in it, but it hangs open anyway.

"Close your mouth before flies get in," Momma says.

After dinner, Daddy turns on the news, and we see a

row of protesters blocking the freeway. It's like a movie instead of real life. It's all smoky, but Daddy tells me it's just exhaust from the cars. And headlights make the protesters look like they're onstage.

Helicopters are high above them. A reporter says the protesters are being warned to get off the freeway.

"Is that illegal?" I ask. "Blocking the freeway like that?"

"Yes," Daddy says. "*Technically*. But sometimes you have to do something that's wrong in some people's eyes but is morally right."

A whole bunch of police cars come onto the freeway, blue and red lights flashing, and they use that lane that's just for emergencies to zoom by all the stopped cars. My hands start to itch.

"Are they going to arrest them?" I ask, but no one answers me.

I get closer to the television to try and see if I can find Hana, but Momma tells me to scoot back so I don't ruin my eyes. My eyes don't seem like the important thing, but I scoot back anyway.

Police officers get into a long line, facing off against the protesters, but the officers have shields in front of them like they're worried that the protesters might hurt them.

I rub my hands on my pants hard, back and forth, back and forth, until Momma kneels next to me and holds my hands, making them quiet.

"They should leave," I say. "They're going to get in trouble."

The smoke thickens, like a blanket of fog is creeping over the freeway, and Daddy says it looks like the police are using tear gas to get the protesters to move.

"What's going to happen?" My voice is wobbly, and my eyes start filling up with tears even though no one shot me with any gas. I wish there was something I could do to help.

I think the police are going to start arresting people, but then the protesters file off the freeway, waving their Black Lives Matter signs, and my heart drops out of my throat and back to where it's supposed to be.

Momma lets go of my hands and tells me to go take my bath.

I want to keep watching the news to make sure nothing else happens, but I know better than to argue.

When I go to bed, Hana still isn't home.

51
Woke

In the morning I knock on Hana's door. I have this awful feeling she won't be there. Like maybe she got arrested or worse. But her sleepy voice croaks, "What?"

I open the door slowly. "Are you okay?" I whisper.

Hana sits up in bed and yawns really big before answering. "I'm fine. Just tired. A bunch of people got arrested, though. They set a car on fire and broke some windows. The police went off."

I take a little gulpy breath. "But they didn't shoot anyone?"

"No, not this time." Hana yawns again. "What do you want?"

I take a step inside. This is risky because Hana doesn't like me to be in her room.

Hana's room is decorated with a big poster from *Love & Basketball* (her favorite movie) and a campaign poster from back when Barack Obama was president. Right next to that is a picture of Colin Kaepernick with his afro shaped into the Black-power fist.

I stare at Hana's poster of two track runners from the Olympics, Tommie Smith and John Carlos, with their fists raised on the winners' platform. They got their medals taken away for protesting. It must've taken a lot of courage to stand in front of all those people and show them fairness is more important than winning a race. I don't think I could ever be that brave.

"*What?*" Hana says, and now her voice doesn't sound sleepy; it sounds exasperated.

"Weren't you scared?" I ask.

"Kind of," Hana says, and I'm surprised because I didn't think Hana ever was afraid. She picks up her armband, which was twisted up like a snake on her bed, and starts pulling it through her fingers. "I mean, I don't want to actually get arrested, you know? But I guess I was more angry than scared. Everybody said that police officer was going to get off just like they always do. I didn't want to believe it, but that's just what happened, and . . . it's like our lives don't matter at *all*. We have to make noise. Wake folks up."

I don't know how to make noise. And I sure don't

know how to not be afraid of getting into trouble. But I want to do *something*.

I watch Hana twisting her armband round and round, and then I look at Kaepernick and at her Olympics poster, and I get an idea. It's an itchy-hands idea. I take a deep breath like I'm about to jump into a pool. "Do you . . . do you have another armband?"

Hana gives me a side-eye, but then she gets out of bed, rustles through her T-shirt drawer, and pulls out a black T-shirt. Then she takes some scissors and cuts the bottom off the shirt. "Here you go," she says.

When I tie it on, I feel . . . proud, even though I know it's not a big deal. It's just an armband. It's not like I'm marching on a freeway. No one will probably even notice that I'm wearing it.

So I don't understand why my hands are seriously itching.

52
All Black

In science, Bernard notices my armband right off, and he asks me about it super loud.

"For BLM," I say. "You know, Black Lives Matter?"

"That jury must've been crazy," Bernard says, still talking too loud.

"You mean crazy *smart*," Howard Michon says. He sits next to me, and I sort of want to sock him.

Even though Mr. Powell warned us that people would have different feelings no matter what the verdict was, I'm still surprised anyone would think that jury made the right decision.

No matter how I slice it, I still get the same lumpy, squashed-up, unfair slice of pie.

Bernard glares at Howard real hard, and you bet Howard doesn't say another word.

"Sit *down*, Bernard," Mr. Levy says.

Then in history, Alex asks about it, and he gives me a high five when I tell him what it's for.

Mr. Powell says that all throughout history people have protested unfair things. He doesn't say the verdict is unfair, but I bet that's what he is talking about. He also says that sometimes things feel like they're getting a whole lot worse before they start to get better.

"Change is hard," he says, rubbing the edge of his scarf.

It sure is. Except maybe for Julia, who is changing all over the place.

Mr. Powell lets us out early, and I'm the first to get to our break spot. It's not until I'm sitting there that I realize Isabella might still be sick, and Julia might not be coming at all.

But then they both turn the corner of one of the portables and join me under the magnolia tree like regular.

I haven't talked to Julia since she stormed off, but neither of us mentions it.

"Why are you wearing that?" Isabella asks, pointing at my armband. She still sounds hoarse.

"Didn't you hear about the verdict?" I ask.

Isabella shakes her head.

It's such a big deal at my house, it never occurred to me that not everybody was on the edge of their seats waiting to see what that jury was going to do. "It's to remind people that Black lives matter because sometimes it seems like that's not what everyone thinks."

"Like you're all Black now?" Julia says, making a snorting sound.

Oh, no she didn't. "What is *that* supposed to mean?"

"You don't even act Black," Julia says, like she knows *all* about it.

Maybe it's all my stored-up hurt feelings, but no way am I going to let Julia get away with saying stuff like that. "What, you think being African American means being ghetto or something? You've known me for *how* long? No matter how I act, I'm still Black, Julia. How would you feel if someone said you had to act a certain way or you wouldn't really be Asian?"

"People do," Julia snaps back. "All the time. Like I have to be so sweet and quiet."

Julia says *sweet* like it's the worst thing anybody could be.

I know people have all sorts of stereotypes about

Asians, but *I* don't. "*I've* never said that," I say. "You've never been quiet." She's also never been all that sweet, but I don't say that.

Isabella holds up her hand for me to give her a high five. "You know that's the truth," she says, and laughs. I think she's probably just trying to make Julia and me stop arguing, but I have to slap her hand anyway.

"I know!" Julia shouts at us, not amused. "Obviously, you guys get me. But people act like they already know all about me just because I'm Asian. And my aunts act like I'm a big disappointment if I'm not perfect all the time!"

"Ha!" Isabella says. "Try being Latinx." Isabella's eyes go wide, like she startled herself. Then she shakes her head. "Seriously, guys. People think we're all Mexican. And that we're probably here illegally. I've never even *been* to Mexico." Isabella frowns, fists her hair together, and wraps it up into a big sloppy bun. She pulls her legs to her chest and rests her chin on her knees. "People are dumb."

Momma tells me I need to look outside myself more. Maybe she's talking about stuff like this. Noticing my friends have problems too. But it seems like I'm the only one who has to worry about someone in my family getting shot. Still, I nod and agree. "Okay. We all have our stuff." Then I lean toward Julia. "So you shouldn't say something like that about me being Black, Jules," I say. "My best friend should know." I have never had trouble saying *best friend* to Julia before.

Then the bell rings.

Instead of sprinting off as usual, Isabella straightens up and sighs. "Shay's right. We all have something, so let's not fight about it, okay?" When neither Julia nor I says anything right away, Isabella says, "Okay?" a little louder and more forcefully.

"Okay!" Julia and I both say at the same time, but neither of us sounds happy about it.

"Good," Isabella says. "I'd make you hug it out, but I gotta go." She shakes her head at both of us before running off.

"Cool?" Julia asks me, and holds out her fist.

"Cool," I say, and bump her fist with mine.

When I get to PE, I have to think about what to do about my armband. I have to take it off to change, but then what? Should I tie it back on? Is it part of my school clothes? Would Coach West have a problem with me wearing it? She's the only Black teacher I have, and I think she'd understand about the armband, but I also don't want it to be a big deal.

I put the armband in my gym locker. But when I see Yolanda, I wish I was wearing it. She doesn't seem happy to see me at all, and I don't want to give up Isabella or Julia, but it would be nice to have a friend who had hair like mine, or knew how it felt for a classroom of kids to stare at you when your teacher decides to show some of the *Roots* miniseries. A friend whose dad listens to old-school R&B and likes to cha-cha in the kitchen and sing about how today was a good day. A friend who knows being Black means all sorts of things. A friend who shares this awful thing, this feeling like maybe the world sort of hates you because of the color of your skin.

"Hi, Yolanda!" I talk loud, trying to show her how happy I am to see her.

"Hi," she says, but she doesn't show me her upside-down Y.

"You've been really into your project in shop." I hope I sound interested and not complainy. She's been so into working hard on her projects that she basically ignores me completely in shop now. I don't know if she thinks I was mean to Tyler, but I really wasn't trying to be. In PE he's not around, so maybe she won't get stuck on that. And she doesn't have a birdhouse or electric wiring to distract her. In PE we can go back to the way it used to be, when it felt like we were becoming friends. At least I hope so.

"I guess," she says. Her head swivels around like she is looking for something or somebody. Somebody who isn't me.

"Your hair looks great today," I say. It's actually not very exciting this time. Just two basic braids, but it's not like I can say that.

Maybe Yolanda knows I was giving her a fake compliment, because she doesn't even say *Thank you*; she just blows air through her teeth.

"Maybe you could come over one day after school?" I say. I'm still smiling really big, even though she isn't smiling at all.

"Oh," she says. "I'd have to ask."

"Okay!" I say, as if she said, *Yes, I'd love to come over and hang out and eat chips and giggle about boys and try your momma's fried chicken and become super good friends*. I'm good at pretending sometimes. I nod and say it again, "Okay!"

Coach West blows her whistle, and we line up to pick teams for softball.

Yolanda is a team captain, and she doesn't pick me even though everybody knows your friend is the absolute first person you should pick. But maybe she doesn't pick me because I strike out a lot.

After English, I walk slowly to our lunch table, the tails of my armband hanging limply down my arm. Ms. Jacobs didn't seem to notice my armband. But she did talk about the next book we were going to read. *To Kill a Mockingbird*. She said it's about a big trial, and the South when it was super prejudiced and racist against Black people (that's not the way she said it) and about people not treating other people fairly. It feels like we're living that story right now, so I don't know if we need to read a book about it.

"What about *Brown Girl Dreaming*?" I said, without meaning to.

Ms. Jacobs looked at me, startled. "Excuse me?"

My neck got hot. I don't usually think out loud. But Daddy's right—there's a whole bunch of perspectives out there we could learn from. "It's just, we could read . . . books by . . . like, other people?"

Ms. Jacobs got a little frowny face, and I'm guessing she's not used to anyone suggesting a different book.

Someone laughed behind me, and I sure wished Ms. Jacobs would stop looking at me. I started picking at my desk. "Black people have things to say too," I said, so softly it was nothing more than a whisper. Thankfully, the bell rang and I was able to escape to lunch.

When I join Isabella and Julia at our table, I look over where Alex stood singing, and think about getting up there and yelling about my life mattering, but I sure don't do it. I twirl the ends of my armband round and round. It feels almost like it's Halloween again and I'm just in a protesting costume.

"Maybe you could bring me an armband," Isabella says, like she knows I'm feeling kind of sad.

"It's for *Black* lives mattering," Julia says.

Isabella shrugs. "Well, I'm *brown*. Seems like that's close enough. And technically, Shayla's brown."

"You don't have to be Black to support Black Lives Matter," I say. Inside I'm wondering, though. Would it be okay for Isabella to wear an armband?

53
Black & Blue

In shop, Yolanda has her head down low over her circuit board and doesn't look up when I take my seat next to her.

I reach over and touch her arm, so softly at first, I don't think she feels it, so I press harder and then she looks up, and asks me *what?* with her eyes and grumpy face.

I swallow hard because I haven't practiced what I'm going to say. "I—I just wanted you to know me and Tyler weren't ever talking," I whisper. "He misunderstood. . . ." I don't want to make it seem like it was all Tyler's fault. "I should've said something sooner. But I straightened it out with him."

A bit of grump slides off of Yolanda's face. She doesn't look mad anymore. She looks like she's listening.

Then she looks at my arm. "What's that for?" she asks.

This isn't something I want to whisper, so I say in a regular voice, "For all the people who've been shot. And for the jury getting it wrong."

Tyler looks over at us, and he's so light-skinned, I can see the blush covering his face. I think he's going to pretend he wasn't listening, so I won't yell at him for butting in, but then he says, "Black lives matter."

Yolanda nods and then totally shocks me by asking me, "Will you bring me one?" She gives me a tiny peek at her upside-down Y.

"Of course." And I decide right then I'll bring one for Isabella too. It'll be nice to have some armband company.

"*Blue* lives matter," a boy at a workbench behind us says. His name is Alvin.

Some people think Black people are against the police because of Black Lives Matter. They think we are saying all police are bad and we hate them. Police wear blue, so saying blue lives matter is like saying blue versus Black. Momma says it's just trying to stir up a mess of trouble. I agree. I don't hate the police. Even Hana doesn't hate the police. Uncle Shelly is a cop, and he's the coolest. So I say, "Of course blue lives matter, stupid."

Mr. Klosner twists his mustache and tells us to get back to work.

Tyler looks at my armband and then down, and I bet he wants to ask me to bring him one, but he doesn't.

When I get changed for track practice, I look at my pile of folded clothes in my gym locker, rub my hands on my thighs, and decide to leave my armband on. Coach West might not like it, but I want to leave it on. It feels important.

Coach West doesn't make me take it off. She nods at it and gives me a thumbs-up. So many people wear them at Black Lives Matter rallies and protests, I'm sure she knows what it's for. I'm glad she's not going to stop me.

During our warm-up mile, the tails of the armband flap behind me, and it makes me feel almost as if I have wings.

Angie runs past me, but then she slows down so I can catch up with her. She smiles at me and points at my armband. "Black lives, right?"

A warm scoop of peach cobbler floats around in my stomach. In my head, I say, "*Yes*, sister." In my head, I say, "Power to the people." In my head, I say, "Let's become really good friends." Out loud, I say, "Right."

Angie runs next to me for the rest of our warm-up, and it feels like when you've been trying and trying to get the two parts of a zipper to fit together at the bottom and are starting to wonder if it's broken because they won't connect, and then suddenly, *whoosh!* they just slide right into place.

Maybe doing something isn't all that hard.

54
Down

The next day I bring Isabella *and* Julia an armband. We are the United Nations and it will feel good to do this together.

At break, I pull two strips of black material out of my pocket.

"Cool," Isabella says, and puts hers on right away.

Julia doesn't take hers.

"What's wrong?" I ask.

"I don't know, Shay. Don't get me wrong. I'm down and everything, but . . ." Julia starts fiddling with her hair. Pulling it back behind her ears and then shaking it back out. Her blue highlights have faded, and now she has streaks of faded yellowish green in her hair. "I'm not sure if it makes sense for us to wear one of those."

Isabella looks down at her own armband. "Huh?"

"You believe that Black lives matter, right?" I ask Julia, still holding out the armband I brought for her. "You know that verdict wasn't fair?" The protests are worse now that the verdict came out. More and more people are shouting for change and shouting for justice. "Don't you think things need to change?" I want her to say that change is important and we're willing to fight for it, even if the fight is just wearing an armband.

"But it's not like wearing it is going to change anything." Julia looks down at the ground, but I can still see her face getting red. "And maybe it's something only the Black kids should do?" She glances over at Isabella and then back down.

"I'm not giving mine back," Isabella says.

I put Julia's armband back in my pocket. "It's cool," I say, trying to act like I don't care. "You don't have to wear one." I'm trying to understand what Julia said, but the truth is, I don't.

It's good I have PE after break, because I give Yolanda an armband and she grins really big at me as she ties it on. I think it's the first true smile I've gotten from her in a really long time. She has black ribbons braided into her braids. I bet she was thinking about matching the armband I was bringing her.

I tell myself that Yolanda being excited about wearing an armband makes up for Julia not taking the armband I brought for her. But I can't make myself believe it.

55
Friendships & Trash Cans

I'm hustling to English, hoping my quick work with a cleansing wipe was good enough to wipe off my PE sweat, when I see a bunch of guys around the trash can outside the cafeteria. Bernard is easy to spot because he's so much bigger than the other guys, and plus he's yelling. Loud.

I'm surprised that no teacher or Principal Trask has gotten over here and stopped this.

I think about skirting around them to get to class, but then I notice Alex in the middle of all those boys, and I can't let Bernard beat up on my friend. Especially when Alex is so much smaller than Bernard.

Even though kids flood the walkway, heading to class, no one seems to be paying attention to what's happening to Alex.

"Bernard!" I yell, and start marching over there. I thought I was wrong about Bernard, but here he is messing with Alex. I don't care how big he is, that's not cool.

One of the boys—Daniel—wraps his arms around Alex, and at first I think he's trying to protect him, but then he lifts Alex off the ground and tries to shove Alex into the trash can. "You think you're so funny," Daniel says. "Let's see you joke about this!"

Most of the boys are laughing, and a few try to grab Bernard's arms, but Bernard is stronger than they are, and he hauls off and punches a guy and then yanks Alex from Daniel.

"You best back off!" Bernard hollers. "You ain't putting Alex in the trash."

I stop in my tracks. Wait. Bernard is *protecting* Alex?

"What are you going to do about it?" a boy named Marcus asks, like he's so tough.

Bernard pushes Alex behind him and then he clobbers Marcus, and that's just when Principal Trask walks outside the cafeteria.

"Bernard Walker!" she shouts, and all the boys freeze. "Why am I *not* surprised?" She glares at Bernard.

"Wait, Principal Trask," Alex speaks up, but I can tell she's not listening to him at all.

"Bernard started it!" one of the boys yells.

"Yeah," Marcus yells, pressing a hand to his eye. "He punched me."

"I can see what was happening here," Principal Trask says.

One of the boys covers his mouth to keep from laughing.

"He started the whole thing," Travis Noen says. Travis is one of those kids who look like they're sweet and innocent, but are always up to something.

"No, that's not—" Alex starts to say, but Principal Trask cuts him off.

"That's enough!" she hollers. "*All* of you," she adds, but she's only looking at Bernard. She shakes her head at him like he is one sorry human and says, "Come with me, Bernard. This is the last straw."

I look at Bernard, waiting for him to defend himself. Waiting for him to explain, but he's just looking at the ground, shuffling his feet back and forth with his hands clenched into fists. My palms start biting at me, and my mouth feels like I sucked on cotton balls. I don't know how many straws Bernard had, but I can't watch him get his last one. "Principal Trask!"

Principal Trask turns her cold blue eyes on me and looks at me like I'm a bug. A bug she's about to squash. "I'm handling something right now."

I cross my arms tight across my chest and say, "You need to listen."

I swear Principal Trask glances at my armband, and then she sniffs and wrinkles her nose like something stinks. "Young lady, do not tell me what I need to do."

Something stinks, all right.

"But you're getting it wrong. Bernard was only protecting Alex." Suddenly, a bunch of mean boy eyes are staring at me, but I don't care. "They were trying to trash Alex, and Bernard stopped them."

Principal Trask's eyes go from Bernard to Alex to the other boys and then back to me. "I seriously doubt—"

"It's the truth!" Alex says, madder than I've ever heard him.

Principal Trask ignores Alex. She takes a step toward Bernard. "Take that off," she says, pointing at Bernard's arm.

Bernard has a black sock tied around his arm. He must've come up with the idea after first period, because

I definitely would've noticed it in science. Especially since this sock is dirty.

"I won't!" Bernard yells, his face and his fists scrunched up tight.

"What did you say?" Principal Trask asks menacingly. As loud as he shouted, she sure heard him, all right. "Take it off."

"I don't have to do what you say!" Bernard booms. "I'm not taking off nothing."

"Just take it off, Bernard," I say. It's not fair, but I don't want to see him get into trouble. Especially when I'm the one who started the whole armband thing.

"I don't want to!" he hollers, but I know it's not me he's mad at.

I don't know what to do, but then Coach West rushes up, all out of breath. "I saw them," she says. "I was coming as fast as I could to help. Shayla's right." She puts her hand on Bernard's back.

Principal Trask's eyes flick between my armband and Bernard's sock like they might just tell her a different story.

Coach West doesn't have to lean down much to be face to face with Bernard. "Maybe you should take that off for now?" Her voice is gentle.

Bernard looks like he's going to cry, and his hands get all fumbly trying to take off the sock, so Coach West helps him.

Travis snickers and Bernard glares at him. You bet Travis's smirk slides right off his face.

Principal Trask wipes her hands together. "Bernard, regardless of the reason, fighting at this school is taken seriously."

Coach West steps forward. "Why don't we discuss this in your office, Dorothy."

Lots of kids have stopped to watch now, and I don't think Principal Trask likes that very much, or maybe she just doesn't like Coach West calling her Dorothy.

"Fine," she says. "All of you come with me." Then she looks at me and Alex. "You both can go to class."

"Are you okay, Alex?" Coach West asks, and he nods. "Why don't you come with us," she tells him. "Make sure we get the whole story."

Principal Trask and the boys walk off. I want to go to Principal Trask's office too, to make sure she listens to Bernard and Alex, but then Coach West tells me, "Don't worry, Shayla, I'll make sure Principal Trask understands. Go ahead and get to class."

On my way to English, I don't think at all about how much trouble I'm going to be in for being late. All I can think about is how Bernard the bully is really Bernard the hero.

When I tell the story at lunch, Julia doesn't believe me. "Are you *sure* he was protecting Alex?"

"Yes," I say, tired of explaining.

"But he's so mean," Julia says.

Isabella says, "Maybe not."

Julia gives me an accusing look. "*You're* the one who said he was going to kill you in science."

"But I was wrong. That's what I'm trying to explain." I don't understand why Julia can't see Bernard in the new light I'm shining right on him.

Julia shrugs. "He's still a bully to me, bruh."

I stare hard at Julia, but I swear it's like I can't see her at all.

Isabella gives a worried frown to her armband. "Trask really made him take off his armband?"

"It was a *sock*," I complain. It's like *no* one's listening to me.

56
Lonely Island

When I see Tyler in shop, I shove the armband I made for Julia into his sweaty hand. "Here," I say.

"Thanks, Shayla!" he says, giving me a big cheesy grin.

"You don't have to sound so surprised," I say, but then I see Yolanda looking at me and I add, "I mean, you're welcome."

By the time I get to track practice, I'm in one of those moods where everything just feels wrong. Angie has on an armband, which should make me happy, but she gives armbands to the other girls she runs the relay race with, and none of them even look my way.

It's like they are all united and I'm on Lonely Island. I'm completely unzipped.

And it sure doesn't help when Coach West makes

me and some of the other girls practice passing the stick with the relay team.

"It's good for you all to know how to do this," she says. "It can be tricky getting the coordination right."

Coach West wasn't lying, because I drop the stupid stick almost every time someone tries to pass it to me, and Natalie sighs each and every time.

When Momma picks me up, she asks me how the day went.

"Fine." I'm not sure if I should tell her about Bernard. If there's one thing Momma hates, it's me and Hana getting in trouble at school. Even though I wasn't the one in trouble, I don't think she'd like that I was even close to it.

"How are you feeling about wearing your armband?"

I don't answer right away, because I don't have a good answer. Yesterday it felt great. But Julia's comment about not being really Black still bugs me. And Principal Trask making it seem like Bernard's armband had something to do with the situation with Alex was pretty awful. Then Angie giving armbands to the relay team like it didn't have anything to do with me—that hurt. "I don't know," I finally say.

"Are you going to keep wearing it?"

Her question surprises me because I hadn't considered not wearing it. I curl the tail between my fingers. Maybe it's not changing anything, but I like wearing it. And I like saying something, even if I'm saying it quietly. "I guess so." I wish that decision would make me feel better, but it doesn't.

When I get home, the first thing I write in my eyeball journal is:

Life STINKS.

And then I write lots more.

Ms. Jacobs said when we turn in our journals, we can paper-clip together any pages we don't want her to read. I will probably have to clip these. I'm not talking to Ms. Jacobs about Julia and how I'm not even sure if we're still friends, or about how I felt connected yesterday but not today, or how wearing an armband was supposed to be a special thing and now I'm not sure. I'm really talking to myself. I can't talk to Isabella, because friends don't talk about other friends behind their backs, and I can't talk to Hana because she will tell me I should've been hanging out with my own in the first place, and Momma would remind me how there is dirty water in Flint, and starving babies in Sudan, and missing girls in Nigeria, and boys getting shot, and those are *real* problems.

My journal doesn't argue or tell me to be more understanding. It just listens.

I wish I hadn't been so scared of Bernard. But it's not like you get to choose what's going to freak you out, right? And if you are never afraid, then how do you know when you're brave?

57
Everyone Hates Us

There's a knock on my door, and I call out, "Come in."

I'm surprised to see Daddy standing there. He hardly ever comes into my room.

"Momma's been calling you to come to the table. Haven't you heard her?"

"Sorry," I say. "I was just really into my homework." I close my observation journal.

"I hear you added a little bit to your wardrobe yesterday." He eyes my armband, and I can't tell if he's happy about it.

"Yeah. I wanted to do something. Show the trial wasn't fair."

"Following in Hana's footsteps, huh?" He smiles at me.

I know Daddy is teasing me, because he knows how

me and Hana both don't like being compared to each other, but I think I hear some pride in his voice too, and that makes me feel all warm inside. "I guess so. Kinda."

Daddy takes a few steps into my room and runs his hand over his hair. He's starting to get one or two gray hairs, and sometimes he tells Momma she should pluck them out for him. "Shayla, I'm proud of what you're doing. It takes courage to stand up for something. Especially at your age."

"Daddy, why do you think that jury said the police officer wasn't guilty? Everybody knows she shot him. Everybody saw the video."

"Why do I get pulled over just because I drive a nice car? Why does Mr. McDonnell keep a closer eye on Black folks when they come into his store? Why is it, every time we—"

I'm not sure what Daddy was about to say because he cuts himself off.

"Look, Shayla, life isn't fair. You're old enough to understand that. And I don't mean just for Black folks. Lots of people aren't treated the way they should be." Daddy pauses and looks around my room like he's trying to find what he wants to say hidden somewhere. "It's just sometimes, it sure seems like Black folks get way too big of a helping of that unfair pie."

I can feel my eyes filling up with tears. "Everyone hates us," I whisper.

"No, Shay. That's not what I'm saying. I know it's hard. All of this is hard. But don't start thinking that."

He spreads his arms as wide as an ocean and I rush right in.

But as he holds me, I can't stop wondering, just what am I *supposed* to think?

58
Divided Nations

On Monday, in science, I give Bernard an armband. He deserves to have a real one.

"That was cool how you stood up for me and all," he says.

"I didn't do anything," I say. "But you did. You didn't let those guys hassle Alex."

He shakes his head. "Makes me mad when folks start messing with Alex. I *had* to pop that dude. Alex is my friend."

"He is?" I don't know why I'm so surprised. Of course Bernard has friends.

"Yeah, we get together and practice our rhymes," Bernard says.

"That's cool," I say, feeling like a complete jerk.

Bernard frowns, and it is the same frown I remember

from elementary school, but it doesn't scare me any-more. It sort of makes him look strong and tough, but *good* tough. "If it hadn't been for you and Coach West, I think Principal Trask would've had me suspended." He ties on the armband. "Thanks."

"Black Lives," I say.

Bernard gives me a hug that feels like he's crushing every rib I have. But I laugh anyway.

"You better sit down," I say.

In second period, this is one of those days when Mr. Powell lets the class out early before break. Well, he lets everyone leave but me.

"Just a minute, Shayla," he says. "I want to talk to you."

My hands start itching immediately. A teacher wanting to talk to you after class is never a good thing. I wonder if it's about our last history test. I thought I had gotten most of the questions right, but you never know. And some of the questions were tricky.

I slowly make my way to his desk.

"Shayla, I've noticed students wearing these arm-bands," he says, pointing at my armband. "They're for Black Lives Matter, right?"

Mr. Powell doesn't say Black students, but that's probably what he means. This morning before school, and going from first to second period, I saw them. Armbands. Even though it's probably because Angie started wearing one, I still think it's pretty cool that it's not just me wearing one.

"Yeah," I say. I think there's probably more I should say, but I'm hoping the armband will do the talking for me.

Mr. Powell nods and plays with the edge of his scarf. It's the one Coach West got for him. Bright purple. "I thought so. I've heard some grumbling that it's not . . . appropriate for students to make political statements at school. What do you think about that?"

My hands start itching. "Are people saying we can't wear them?"

"No, I haven't heard anyone say that. People can get scared with anything that challenges the status quo. But standing up for what you believe in is important. I just wanted you to be prepared, in case someone says something to you."

I feel like Mr. Powell is trying to warn me, but I'm not sure about what, and before I can work my courage up to ask him, the bell rings.

"Thank you, Shayla," he says. "Go ahead and get to break."

I grab my books and head out into the hallway. It's already packed with people, and instead of pushing my way through the crowd like I normally do, I sort of just let it carry me along. Like I'm a piece of driftwood caught in a current.

Last night, there was another huge protest about the verdict. Hana told me about it. She said protesters stood outside the house of the police officer who got off. They wouldn't leave, and a bunch of people were arrested. Even one of Hana's friends got arrested, but he got let go a few hours later.

What that jury decided was wrong. You can't be afraid of someone just because they're Black. You can't just shoot someone because they're Black. But the protests scare me.

When I get to our break spot, I'm glad to see Isabella is wearing her armband again today. We fist-bump each other.

"Guess what!" Isabella squeals, clasping her hands together. "My mom said I could get a kitten!"

"You're so lucky," I say, feeling a flash of jealousy. But

it's just a camera flash. A second that goes away as fast as it came. "I can't wait to play with him. Maybe I can come over this weekend?" It feels weird to say *I*, and not *we*.

Isabella snatches one of my carrots and leans back on her elbows. She smiles up at the sun. "Totally."

Neither of us says anything about Julia not showing up.

After English, I slowly make my way to my locker to get my lunch. I want to give Julia plenty of time to get to our table first. I spin the little dial, in full jewel-thief mode, and get a little thrill when I pop the locker open. I am so ready for a life of crime. I get out my lunch, push my locker closed, and then lean against it for a minute, watching everyone hustle by. After a few minutes the hallway is empty, and I push off my locker and head outside.

Isabella is at our table, but Julia isn't.

Isabella glances over at another table, and I follow her gaze, knowing what I'll see.

Julia's sitting three tables over with her other friends. Isabella's eyes go wide, and she opens her mouth to say something, but instead she shoves a big handful of grapes into her mouth. I sit across from Isabella and slowly take out my lunch.

This feels different. Different bad. Because she's right *there*. Making a choice.

The Pacific Ocean is between us. The Sahara Desert. We are not the United Nations. We're the Divided Nations. And there's nothing cute about that nickname.

I wonder if she's sitting over there because of the armbands. I sure hope not.

Isabella swallows. "We should say something, right?"

"What would we say?" I ask.

Julia looks over and smiles. Maybe to say, *See, everything's cool.*

Everything is not cool, but I try my best to smile back. I glance at Isabella, and she doesn't smile. She bites off a hangnail and spits it on the ground.

I try my best to think this is no big deal. I guess Isabella and I could go over there, but *we* are in *our* lunch spot. It doesn't seem like we should have to chase Julia down so we can all stick together.

When lunch is almost over, Julia comes to the table. "All my friends want an armband!"

She doesn't say she's sorry for not sitting with us. She

doesn't *look* sorry. And I sure don't like the way she said *all my friends*.

"Whatever, Julia."

Julia doesn't get the hint. "Stacy said us all wearing them is gonna be *lit*!"

"I don't have enough material to make armbands for all of them," I say.

Julia stares at me for a second. "You wanted me to wear one. Now you don't?"

Isabella rubs the fabric of her armband. "You guys could probably make them." She shrugs, like it's no big deal if they do or don't, but she kicks me under the table.

I kick Isabella back and glare at her. I don't want her helping them; I want her to be mad at Julia with me.

"Okay, coolio," Julia says.

She sounds like a big phony. "It's not supposed to be a fun thing," I say pointedly. "It means something."

"I *know*," Julia says, and raises an eyebrow at me. "Don't get it twisted, Shay."

"I'm not twisting anything." I crumple up my lunch bag even though it still has an orange in there. I get up and shove the bag into the trash.

"Forget it," she says to my back. "We'll make our own."

"Great," I say.

A whole bunch of people suddenly run by, shouting "Fight! Fight!"

"Let's go see!" Julia says, right as the bell rings.

A fight means trouble, so when Julia follows the group going left, I head right.

59
Something Smells

I put my math book into my locker, and this time I shut it with a very satisfying slam before I see Principal Trask. She gives me a disapproving look, and her nose wrinkles up. We had to run the mile in PE today, so at first I worry I might stink, but then I realize Principal Trask is staring hard at my armband.

In fifth period I found out the fight was all about Noah Randolph getting commanded to take off his armband and he wouldn't, so a bunch of other boys started whaling on him.

The way I heard it, by the time Principal Trask waded in, one boy had a bloody nose and Noah had a puffy eye. And even though Noah wouldn't take off his armband, it ended up being torn off anyway and Principal Trask made him throw it away.

Hearing about that fight made me nervous about wearing an armband, even though I'm not even playing Command.

But now I think about what Mr. Powell told me about some people not liking us wearing armbands, and I figure Principal Trask must agree because her face sure is frowny. Which is straight-up wrong because they don't have a thing to do with her.

Still, with her little vein-lined nose all wrinkled up, I sort of wish I wasn't wearing my armband right now. I can't help but remember when she made me take off my costume at Halloween.

When she told Bernard to take off that sock he was wearing, he said no. I don't know if I could be brave enough to do that.

But all she says is, "You're going to be late for class."

I run all the way to shop.

60
Dress Codes &
Disciplinary Action

Principal Trask's voice booms out from the PA in shop.

"Attention, students!" her high-pitched voice says. "Please be informed that while we understand wanting to support . . . people . . . in the community. . . , the wearing of armbands is against school-policy dress code. All armbands need to be removed. Failure to do so will be met with disciplinary action."

I hear someone snicker in the back of class, and I turn real quick to see who it is, but I don't catch them.

I touch my armband. It makes me feel strong. I don't want to take it off. I look over at Yolanda and her eyes look scared. Neither of us knows what to do.

Mr. Klosner tells everyone to get back to work on their projects.

Alvin points at my armband while I'm waiting to

use the table saw. "You're supposed to take that off," he says.

I shrug.

"Take off that armband," Alvin says again.

"Make me," I say, and shove my fists onto my hips.

Alvin is about five inches shorter than me, and he's as scrawny as a chicken wing. He blinks a bunch of times and walks away. I guess he doesn't need to use the table saw after all.

Just what sort of disciplinary action was Principal Trask talking about?

61
Tangles

Momma is rubbing coconut oil into my hair and combing out the tangles, and let me tell you, it is one good feeling having your scalp rubbed.

Today has felt as tangled as my hair. I sure wish there was a way to comb through it all. I didn't tell Momma about Principal Trask's announcement because I haven't decided what I'm going to do yet. I know I don't want to stop wearing my armband.

Then Daddy walks into my room.

"There's been another shooting," he says, and Momma forgets to be gentle and yanks my hair hard.

"Ow!" I say. For a second, maybe more than a second, I think he is saying Hana has been shot. For a second, maybe more than a second, I can't breathe.

"What happened?" Momma asked.

"A Black woman was selling incense in front of a store," Daddy said. He speaks real quiet and slow. "Someone called the police even though according to the store owner, there weren't any problems. And when the police got there—" Daddy's voice breaks and he runs a hand over his head.

Momma and I wait for him to find his way.

He lets out a long slow breath. "Two officers shot her," he says. "They've been talking about it on the news."

"Why did they shoot her?" I ask. "What was she doing wrong?"

"Not a damn thing," Daddy says.

"Richard," Momma says. She doesn't let any of us swear. Not even Daddy.

But Daddy repeats what he said.

"Lord, Lord," is all Momma says. She rubs more oil into my hair.

"When is this going to stop?" Daddy asks, but I don't think he's asking me or Momma the question.

"Is there a video?" Momma asks.

Daddy sucks his teeth. "Like that's going to make a difference?"

My head feels heavy like there are bricks sitting on top. That video sure didn't help in the trial, so I know what Daddy means. I wonder if Principal Trask had already heard about the shooting when she decided to ban armbands.

"We'll get through this," Momma says. "That's what we do."

She pats the top of my head, letting me know she's done, and then she gives me a kiss and tells me to get into bed.

She follows Daddy out of my room, and I know they are going to be up late talking about this.

I'm tired but I can't sleep. I keep tossing and turning and looking for that comfortable spot, but it's hiding from me. I creep out of bed and go to Hana's room.

Her music is so loud coming out of her headphones, I can hear it across the room, but she turns it off so I can talk to her.

"Principal Trask said we have to stop wearing the armbands. She said it's a dress-code violation." I say that last bit super sarcastic so Hana can know right away that my principal is being unfair.

"Yeah, I was wondering when that was going

to happen," Hana says. She looks up at the picture of Kaepernick. "Folks aren't about to let any type of protest go down without trying to stop it. Guess they think that's better than fixing the actual problem."

"But it's not fair! She shouldn't be able to do that." I feel sort of like crying and also like punching something.

"So what are you going to do about it?" Hana asks.

"I don't want to stop wearing it," I say. "Especially not now."

"Then don't."

I know wearing an armband hasn't changed anything, but I can't stop wearing it now.

I really don't want to get into trouble, though.

62
Take a Stand

In the morning, my palms are itching so bad, it's hard to tie my armband on. I don't think I have ever done something I know one hundred percent is going to land me in a whole heap of stinky trouble. And part of me is trying to tell the other part that it is sort of silly. I'm not going to keep anybody from getting shot just by wearing an armband. But the louder part of me is saying that people need to start paying attention. I tie another knot in my armband, making sure it's good and tight.

Hana raises her fist and winks at me as I'm heading out of the house, and I raise my fist too. She looks proud of me, and that feels like maple syrup sliding down my throat.

On the way to school, Momma has the car radio turned to a news station, and they're talking about a big Black

Lives Matter protest happening in front of the Wilshire Community police station. That's right by my aunt Yvonne's house. Momma's hands get really tight on the steering wheel, but she doesn't change the station.

I twirl the tail of my armband. I still haven't told Momma about Principal Trask saying we couldn't wear armbands anymore. I'm not sure if Momma would be mad or proud of me. But I guess I'll find out.

I put my sweater on when I go into school, because I don't want Principal Trask to see my armband before I even get to first period.

Science is loud because Mr. Levy is fiddling with a plastic skeleton and not paying attention to us. Even though the bell already rang, lots of kids are up talking.

Bernard comes over to my desk and towers over me. I can't tell if he's smiling or scowling, and I realize he just has one of those faces.

He's wearing the armband I gave him, and I can't help but worry about that. "Do you think you should take that off? So you don't get into trouble?"

Bernard looks at his armband, then back at me. "Did you take yours off?"

I pull off my sweater and smile. "Nope."

"Some stuff it's okay to get in trouble for," he says, and shrugs.

Maybe when you get in trouble enough times, it stops scaring you, but my hands are itching so bad, I have to rub them hard against my jeans.

"Bernard, take your seat," Mr. Levy says, sounding super exasperated.

Suddenly, I'm tired of how Mr. Levy seems to pick on Bernard, and even though my hands are itching even more, I say loud enough for Mr. Levy to hear, "Other people are up too."

Mr. Levy looks at me like he's never seen me before.

"You better sit down," I tell Bernard.

Bernard frowns, but he goes to the back of the room and squeezes into his desk.

63
Rules

"I thought those were against the rules," Isabella says, nodding at my armband. She's not wearing hers and I'm not mad about it, but I sort of wish she still had it on.

"That's what Principal Trask said," I say. I reach into her bag of Cheez-Its and take a couple.

Isabella doesn't say anything for a second. She's probably wondering if body snatchers took the real Shayla away or something, because she knows how I feel about getting into trouble.

But so far, it doesn't seem like that big of a deal at all that I decided to wear my armband. I'm almost a little disappointed.

I don't know what I expected. Not police dogs or anything, but when I saw it wasn't just me who decided to break the no-armband rule today, I *did* have visions of all of us rule-breaking, armband-wearing students getting rounded up. But nothing's happened.

Isabella and I go our separate ways after break, and I think how weird it is that it's not all that weird for it to be just Isabella and me.

In fourth period, right before lunch, Principal Trask comes back on the PA to remind us about dress-code violations.

Ms. Jacobs sighs, and then she looks at the Emerson quote about being on your own path. And *then* she gives me a teeny nod.

I guess Emerson wasn't talking about armbands, but I think he was talking about doing something brave.

My armband is staying on.

When I sit down for lunch, I make myself not even look over at Julia sitting with her other friends. If she doesn't miss me, I don't miss her.

Isabella says maybe I should take the armband off, but I shake my head hard, and then I see Principal Trask heading over to the basketball courts. She is holding scissors.

I get up right away and follow her, and Isabella follows me. A bunch of other people leave the lunch area too to see what's going on.

Even though Principal Trask is holding those scissors

out like a sword, I'm still shocked when she starts cutting off people's armbands. I don't get close enough to hear what everyone's saying, but I can tell that there are lots of angry voices. Principal Trask doesn't look like she cares one bit that people are upset about her cutting off their armbands; she just keeps snipping.

I put my hand over my armband as if she's about to cut mine off too, but I'm too far away for her to even notice.

"That's so messed up," Isabella whispers.

I'm not sure what to do, because I want to go over there and show I'm part of the armband-wearing group, but if I do, it will mean my armband will get cut off.

"Come on," I say to Isabella. "Let's go back."

When we return to our table, Julia catches my gaze, and her eyes are full of concern just like mine.

For the rest of lunch, I wait for Principal Trask to come over to the overhang lunch area and cut off armbands from everyone who's still wearing them, but she doesn't. It sort of makes me feel sick that she only went over to the basketball courts, like she thinks Black students are the problem.

After school, I'm kicking pinecones while waiting

for Momma to pick me up. I'm kicking them really hard. I wanted, just this once, to get into trouble. But then I didn't. I probably should've gone over to the basketball courts. I wish I had been braver.

And then Principal Trask walks right by me.

And then she backs up.

Like maybe she can't believe her eyes.

"Young lady," she says, "I am sure you heard my announcements about the dress code."

I look down at what I'm wearing, like I have no clue what she's talking about. My palms are itching but I barely feel it. "I'm obeying the dress code," I say, my voice wobbly.

She blinks at me. She points to the armband. "That is against dress code."

"I don't think—" I start to say, but I'm not sure exactly what is going to follow those words, and it doesn't matter because Principal Trask cuts me right off.

"What is your name?"

"Shayla," I say. "Shayla Willows."

"Aren't you on the track team?"

"Yes."

"Well, Shayla, if you want to stay on the team, make

sure I don't see that tomorrow." And then she walks off.

Momma pulls up right then, and when I get in the car she asks me what Principal Trask wanted.

"Nothing," I say. "Just making sure I had a ride." I didn't *plan* to lie to Momma. And let me tell you, lying is probably the worst thing you can do in my family. Talk about trouble! But I know I'm going to wear my armband tomorrow, and I can't let Momma stop me before I have the opportunity to truly protest.

Tomorrow I'm going to find out just what big trouble feels like. For real.

Today I felt like I was a part of something and apart from it at the same time.

64
Go Down Big

In the morning, Hana hands me a bag. It is full of black armbands.

"If you're going to go down," she says, "go down big."

I swallow the sour-apple lump lodged in my throat and rub my hands hard against my legs.

I will be super sad to be off the track team. But there isn't one thing about armbands in the school handbook. Principal Trask is wrong.

I ask Momma if she will drop me off to school early so I can take care of a special project.

I wait for her to ask what the project is, but she just looks at her watch and says, "Oh, sugar, that would actually help me out a lot."

When she drops me off, she gives me a quick kiss on the cheek. "See you after school."

Maybe I should feel guiltier for not telling Momma what I'm up to, but I'm hoping she'll understand.

Since it's early, only a few kids stand around in front of the school. They'll be my first targets.

"Black Lives Matter!" I shout to get their attention. And then I start handing out armbands.

Except for one girl, they all take one. This is going great.

A few minutes later, more students come, and I shove an armband into everyone's hand. I keep hollering, "Black Lives Matter," and some other people join in. I wish I'd made signs. I wish I had my phone to video this.

Isabella gets dropped off, and she giggles when she sees me. She holds out her hand for an armband like it's a party favor. "This is awesome, Shay!"

"This is *important*, Is," I say, giving her an armband.

Julia and her whole squad stopped wearing their armbands yesterday, but today they get new ones. Stacy gives me a high five and says, "You know what I'm talking about, sister." I can't even be mad because I'm so happy that they all want one of my armbands.

Sometimes it's like the world is telling us that being

Black is the worst thing you can be, but right now it feels like people are not only saying that Black lives matter, but that being Black is the best. My smile is so big, it hurts.

Julia smiles at me as she takes an armband. "Thanks, Shay."

Angie asks for a handful just as the bell rings for first period. We all start heading inside. A bunch of Emerson students of all different races are shouting that Black lives matter. I don't care that not *everyone* took an armband. It just feels great to be united.

"Shayla Willows!" Principal Trask's voice booms like she has a microphone. "Give me that bag."

I throw the bag to Angie, who runs up the pathway and through the silver front doors of our school. Man, that girl is fast.

"What bag?" I ask Principal Trask.

She tugs at my armband. "These are expressly forbidden!"

I hear a ripping sound, and then Principal Trask is standing there holding *my* armband. I've never been so mad. "Give that back!"

Principal Trask bends down a little so we are face

to face. "I want you to go around and take back every armband you passed out. If you don't, I will see you in my office and your parents will be called. Being off the track team is just the beginning." Her breath smells like black licorice, which is maybe one of the nastiest smells ever.

I take a step back and feel a bad quivering in my bottom lip. My nose starts burning. I don't want Principal Trask to see me cry.

"Did you hear me, Miss Willows?"

"Yes." It is just one word, but it sounds a whole lot like defeat. Momma always told me and Hana we had to act better than other kids because people expected less of us. Getting called to the principal's office is definitely not acting better. "Principal Trask, it's our right to protest."

"I expect my rules to be followed." Principal Trask is so sure I'm not going to argue, she marches off without waiting for me to say anything else.

I don't know what to do.

After science, Bernard asks me if I want him to take off his armband so I won't get into trouble. And I almost say yes.

Almost.

"No," I say. "Do you think you can find me another one?" I sure hope there is at least one left in the bag.

I don't know what is going to happen, and my palms itch, but I can't worry about that.

Mr. Powell tells me to wait after class, and I'm nervous all over again that he's going to tell me this is what he warned me about and I better stop messing up.

"Shayla, I just wanted to let you know I'm proud of you. It takes courage to stand up for what's right." He smiles at me, but then his smile slips. "You know, there are times when people want me to feel bad about who I am," he says, and sighs. "But I am who I am. I'm not about to apologize for it. I wear bright scarves even though I know some people make fun of them."

I wish I could argue with him, but it's true. Some people do make rude comments.

Mr. Powell's smile returns, and he straightens up tall. "But hey, *I* like them. It's a small thing, but I hope some students may realize it's okay to be different."

"It's not anyone's business what you wear," I say.

Mr. Powell winks at me and says, "I think you're absolutely right." Then he puts his hand out for a fist bump.

Mr. Powell is so cool.

Instead of going to our spot, Isabella and I just walk around at break, and I see so many people wearing armbands, I get those busy butterflies in my stomach. Angie finds me and gives me back my bag. It is almost empty, but there are a few armbands left. I put one on right away and Isabella helps me pass out the rest.

I don't see Principal Trask, and I bet it's because she knows she is totally outnumbered. But she also knows I'm the one who passed out all those armbands, and I don't think she's going to forget about me.

Yolanda flashes me a big upside-down-Y smile in PE, and when Coach West makes me Rebels team captain for Star Wars tag, I pick Yolanda first for my team.

In English, Ms. Jacobs is just finishing writing a new quote on the board when I walk in.

You may shoot me with your words,
You may cut me with your eyes,
You may kill me with your hatefulness,
But still, like air, I'll rise.
　　　　　—Maya Angelou

Then she reads Maya Angelou's whole poem out loud. The poem is called "Still I Rise," and even though

Ms. Jacobs is staring at me like she read the poem just for me, I don't shrink low in my seat. I straighten up tall and proud. I smile at Ms. Jacobs, and she gives me a small smile back. I'm going to print out a copy of Maya Angelou's poem when I get home and stick it right up on my wall.

65
Show Me

Lunch is wild.

We march around the lunch area, and around the track, and by the basketball courts, chanting "Black Lives Matter!" and it feels awesome. And I feel like we matter, for real. A bunch of teachers watch, but none of them stop us.

I'm not sure why so many people wear my armbands. Maybe it's just the excitement of breaking the rules. Or maybe it's because a lot of us know we won't have many chances to shout out loud that we matter.

Coach West claps for us when we're marching and waves at me, and that's when I see she is wearing a black armband too.

And then someone taps me on the shoulder.

"Come with me, young lady," a very angry voice says, right into my ear.

Principal Trask's mouth is so firm and sharp, we could use it in shop as a saw.

I follow her to the office, and before we go into the building, I hear someone shout, "Free Shayla!" That makes me smile.

You bet I stop smiling when Principal Trask tells me she's called Momma, though.

"She'll be here in a few minutes," Prinipal Trask says, and points to a chair right outside her office. "Sit here and wait, please."

I sit.

I am in so much trouble. I didn't know how much I loved being on the track team until now. And I threw it away. Worse, I've let Momma and Daddy down. They've told me and Hana over and over again how important it is that we stay out of trouble in school. My hand travels to my armband, and even though part of me feels like someone punched me in the stomach, a tiny bit of that proud feeling I had a few minutes ago tingles in my fingers. Still, my eyes start brimming with tears.

When Momma walks in and I see the big frown on her face, I stand up on trembly legs and follow her into Principal Trask's office.

But unbelievably, Momma's frown isn't for me.

"I want you to show me right now where in the dress code it says anything about armbands," she tells Principal Trask, slapping the *Ralph Waldo Emerson Junior High Handbook* hard on the desk.

I wipe my tears away.

"That's hardly the point," Principal Trask says.

"That is absolutely the point," Momma says. "You told me my daughter was breaking the dress code. Show me that in this here book. Go ahead, show me."

Momma's voice is loud. Really loud. I know Principal Trask would never believe how sweet Momma can be and how much she hates to use her angry voice.

"We can't have children disrespecting—"

"Excuse me? Disrespecting whom? Because as far as I can see, they are showing a huge amount of respect for the victims who have lost their lives. Don't you think that's important?"

I want to cheer for Momma, but I stay quiet.

"The armbands have become a distraction," Principal Trask says.

I can't keep quiet anymore. "But Principal Trask, that's the *point*." I stop rubbing my hands on my pants. "To make people take notice. It could change things."

Principal Trask stares out the window for a moment. Then she looks at me. She looks at Momma. "If we can agree that the bands shouldn't be worn during school hours—"

"No, ma'am," Momma says. "We can*not* agree on that. There isn't one thing wrong with these students showing that they understand the value of life. That's just what this school should be teaching. Have you ever read any of Ralph Waldo Emerson's works?"

I didn't realize that Principal Trask could get that pale. "I think this maybe just got a little out of hand." She rearranges the files on her desk, lining them up perfectly.

Momma nods. And then she does something I sure don't like. She turns to me and says, "Now, Shayla, I want you to apologize to your principal for not bringing this issue to her in the correct way."

Momma can't possibly want me to say I'm sorry! But I can tell by her frown that that's exactly what she wants. And I remember something Daddy told me. *Don't ever leave your enemies empty-handed. Give them a bone to gnaw on or they will keep on trying to bite you.*

"I'm sorry," I mumble. I just know Momma is going

to make me repeat it louder, but instead, she nods. Satisfied.

Principal Trask looks like she has put too many olives in her mouth and has no idea what to do with the pits. Finally, she says to Momma, "I do appreciate you coming in."

Momma signs me out of school for the rest of the day, and I wait all the way until we're at the car before I raise my hands above my head like I'm a champion.

"Yes!" I shout. "We did it!" I can hardly believe I get to keep wearing my armband *and* stay on the track team.

Momma laughs at me, and then we go get ice cream. "Proud of you, baby," she says as we find seats outside. "You did good."

I look down at my ice cream and feel the *I know* look I wanted steal over my face. I bet feeling good about yourself for being brave feels tons better than something silly like having a boyfriend.

When we get home, Momma gives me back my phone.

The first thing I do is post a selfie of me wearing my armband.

Julia sends me a picture of her, me, and Isabella from

our last day at elementary school. She only has two words in her text message: **United Nations**.

As Momma would say, getting that message has me all up in my feelings.

I never knew walking right into trouble would make me feel strong. Maybe it has to be the right type of trouble.

66
Fumbling &
Stumbling

Today is our last track meet, and I'm a little nervous.

It's not about wearing my armband, because after Momma's visit, Principal Trask hasn't said one word on the PA about dress-code violations.

And it's not the whole face-plant-on-the-track thing. I've actually been jumping the hurdles okay at our meets and have established a good rhythm. I still clip a hurdle sometimes, but I haven't fallen again—at least not at a meet. I'm steady coming out of the blocks now too, so it's all starting to come together. Figures I'd start getting good with hurdles right when the season is about over.

Momma and Daddy are sitting right there in the stands ready to watch me run, after promising they'd stay away, but that's not what's making me so anxious either.

It must be who we're facing today, because our whole team is bursting with nervous energy. Everyone is hyped. We're racing against John Wayne Junior High—they're our main competition.

If we beat John Wayne, we'll end the season first place in our district.

Runners for the 200 are called to the track, and I stop doing my high-kick warm-ups to watch. Carmetta passes by me on her way to line up, and I give her a high five. I know how fast she is. I figure she should win easy.

The gun pops and the girls take off. Carmetta stumbles but catches herself and keeps running. After the first fifty meters I can tell something is wrong with her. She is in last place. I start whispering, "Come on, Carmetta, come on," but she runs even slower. By the time she gets to the finish line, she is limping and crying. There is a hush on our side of the bleachers as everyone watches Coach West go over to her. Coach West talks to Carmetta for a while, feeling her leg and her ankle. I hold my breath, because I know Coach West has a way of fixing things. I'm sure she'll blow that whistle of hers and Carmetta will pop up and do fist pumps. But that doesn't happen.

Coach West has to help Carmetta up. Then Carmetta uses Coach West as a crutch and hobbles over to the sidelines.

They announce it's time for the hurdles. I'm so

caught up in thinking about Carmetta, I forget to be worried and just run my race.

Wait. I do not just run my race. I run my best race ever. I probably have my best start, getting out of the blocks fast and clean, and I don't clip a single hurdle. I don't beat Angie, but I hold on to second place, which for me is completely awesome. After the race, Coach West comes over to talk to me.

"You did great out there, Shayla," she starts.

I figure she wants to tell me how proud she is of me, but she wants to talk to me about Carmetta.

Coach West says Carmetta has sprained her ankle really bad. Which means she isn't going to be able to compete in the girls' relay. Which means someone is going to have to take her spot. My palms start to itch.

"So, Shayla, do you think you could help us out?" Coach West asks, like it is no big deal. Like I can say yes or no, and it will be fine either way.

But if I say no, it means we'll have to scratch the race. How can I say no? But if I say yes, it means I'll have to survive receiving and handing off the baton. And I'll also have to run a hundred meters, really, really fast. Maybe I should've let Principal Trask kick me off the track team.

As if she's reading my mind, Coach West says, "We'll have you run the second leg. Angie is going to take anchor, and Maya will stay in third." She pauses. "Natalie will lead off." I wonder if she is thinking about all the times Natalie dropped the baton at practice. But Natalie is fast. Almost as fast as Angie, who usually runs the lead leg because she always gives our team a good head start. I hope Natalie can do the same.

Coach West looks at me encouragingly. "This is why I make *all* you girls practice passing the baton," she says.

I hated those practices. All the fumbling, and stumbling, and batons slipping and dropping to the ground. Did Coach West remember how much I struggled with that stupid aluminum tube? Track batons are slippery, especially if your palms are itchy when you're trying to grab one.

But either she doesn't remember or she's desperate, because she says, "You know how, Shayla. You can do it. You're doing great with your events, and you know I always tell you you're faster than you realize."

My head says *no*, but for some reason, my mouth says, "Okay."

67
Stick

When they hear I'm going to run, Angie and Maya both give me hugs, but Natalie just nods at me.

I follow them to the grass to stretch. As scared as I am to run, it feels good to sit with them and stretch together.

When the announcer calls the two-minute warning for our race, the other girls pull me into a four-way huddle. I have watched them do it before every race.

"Y'all know we got this thing, right?" Natalie says, looking directly at me.

"We sure do!" Maya and Angie say. I just nod.

"We didn't hear you, Willows! Do we got this thing?" Natalie shouts at me.

Is she mad at me, or just mad that Carmetta can't run? "Yeah," I croak, but then I swallow hard and say,

"Yeah, we got this!"

We put our hands together and say, "Team!"

I line up at my spot, and it feels odd to be just standing there, not in blocks and not facing down hurdles. I hear the gun and then I shut everything out. Waiting for Natalie. She is coming fast. Maybe too fast.

When she starts to get close, I start running with my itchy hand stuck out behind me, hoping and praying we'll connect.

We have to make the transfer before I'm out of the handoff zone. If I get it late, we'll be disqualified.

"Stick, stick!" Natalie screams at me.

I'm nearing the end of the zone. I feel the baton in my hand, but Natalie's not letting go and the baton is bobbling. I feel it slip. I'm losing it! But then my hand closes around it tight, and then I'm running as fast as I can. I don't even want to think about passing it to Maya. I just run, and I see Maya standing there, ready. And then she starts running, with her hand out behind her, ready for me to pass the baton.

"Stick," I say, passing the baton cleanly into her hand. I run a few more meters and then stop, my hands on my knees, breathing hard. It seems like we are way behind. I lost us some ground. I'm scared to watch the rest of the race, but I have to. Natalie runs up behind me and squeezes me in a hug.

"You saved my butt, girl!" she says.

I shake my head. We are a team. We watch together as Maya gains on the girl ahead of her, and we both hold our breath when Maya hands off to Angie. The pass is perfect. Angie runs faster than I've ever seen her go. Carmetta is suddenly next to us, and we all are screaming, "Go, Angie, go!" And then Maya joins us too.

Angie is still in second, and the Wayne girl seems like she is going to be too fast to catch. But Angie is gaining on her, and I feel a scream get caught in my throat. Then they're neck and neck, and the finish line is right in front of them.

When Angie crosses the finish line first, we scream like we are on fire. Angie keeps running until she joins us, and we all jump up and down and shout and pat each other on the back and give high fives. (Of course, Carmetta doesn't jump up and down with her hurt ankle and all, but her spirit is jumping. I can tell.)

And then I get this idea, and I stick my fist high up in the sky. Angie smiles and put hers up too. Then Natalie and Maya and Carmetta. And for just a second we are Olympic athletes saying we matter as much as anybody.

Coach West comes over and gives us a group hug. She always tells us she doesn't care if we win or lose, but I've noticed she's *much* happier when we win. She pats me on the shoulder. "Thanks for helping us out," she says. It seems weird that she is thanking me, because it really feels like I should be thanking her for something.

Winning felt awesome, but being part of the team? That was even better.

68
Almost Over

It's hard to believe that my first year of junior high is almost over. Maybe because we still have Easter decorations up at home. I tell you, Momma being a student has not improved our home life. I have to do my own laundry now, and once a week, Hana and I have to cook dinner. Sometimes I want to remind Momma that I'm only twelve, but I know she would just think that is too funny.

Isabella came over after school today so we could pretend to study vocabulary words. What we are really doing is eating chips and gossiping in my room.

I grab some chips, and with my mouth full I say, "I've been thinking."

"About?"

"We have loads of time before we start dealing with

the whole boy thing, right?" I can't believe I risked a friendship over a boy.

Isabella looks around the room like there might be a hidden camera or something. "Uh, where did Shayla go?" she asks.

I grin at her and wiggle my eyebrows. "Seriously," I say. "I acted stupid over Jace. I'm not going to do that again. And I'm going to *try* to not be so jealous about how pretty you are."

Isabella drops her head, letting her hair fall into her face. "You're so weird." But then she looks at me and I can see trouble twinkling in her eyes. "Next time you go crazy over a boy, you know who it should be?"

"Who?"

"Alex!"

"*What?*" I ask, and start laughing at how ridiculous that is, and then Isabella is laughing too, and we both can't stop, and I almost feel like I'm going to pee my pants.

There's a knock on my door, and I choke out, "Come in," between giggles and snorts.

The door slowly opens, and Julia is standing there looking a little . . . scared.

69
Hard Laughter

Isabella and I immediately stop laughing like we've been caught doing something bad.

"Come in! Jeez, you don't have to knock," I say.

Julia nods. "Yeah, I know." She walks in and stands in the middle of my room, as if it is the first time she has ever been there. "So, what's so funny?"

"Oh, nothing," I say, which is sort of worse than explaining.

Julia plops down on my beanbag chair and starts playing with the rough seam that always scratches you whenever you move. "I saw on Instagram that you were both here."

I feel guilty right away. Momma is always telling me it's not nice to post a picture when it might hurt someone's feelings. But honestly, it didn't even occur to me that Julia would care that Isabella and I are hanging out without her. "I would've texted you to come over, but . . ."

"Yeah, I know." She rubs at the seam and keeps her head down. And then she looks right at me. "I miss you guys."

I'm totally shocked. I've missed Julia so much this year, but it never seemed like she was missing us. "I miss you too."

"We both do," Isabella says.

Julia gets up and starts messing with stuff on my desk. I see her look at the cover of my eyeball journal, and I hope she won't start paging through it. Some of the things in there about her aren't all that nice. She stares up at the poster of Tommie Smith and John Carlos with their fists raised at the Olympics—the same one Hana has in her room. She glances at my bulletin board with all our pictures, and then she turns around and faces us. "When I said it wasn't a big deal me not being around, I knew it wasn't true," she says. "It was a big deal, but I didn't want to admit it. And I didn't know what to do. It was fun being with a group who gets that Japanese and Chinese and Korean and everything aren't the same thing. And that being Asian doesn't mean being a certain way. Like being sweet, or quiet."

"I get that," Isabella says. "People think Latinx is what they see in movies. Illegals and gang members. And they act like Puerto Rico isn't part of this country. Like with the hurricane? We still haven't gotten the help to rebuild like we should've. And we're as American as anybody."

Julia sighs. "Yeah."

It feels like things are finally getting back to normal, and I don't want to ruin it, but I need to say something. "We all know what it's like to be treated wrong, just because of the way we look, but . . ." I pause, trying to get the words to come out right. "But when people make assumptions about *you*, no one dies."

Both of my friends look at me with wide eyes, and it takes a second but then I can tell they both get it. Maybe that was the thing I needed most, for my friends to understand.

We're quiet for a minute and Julia seems really sad now.

"Hey," I say to her, my voice serious. She looks at me, and I can tell she's nervous. "Just so you know, we never would've been best friends if you were *quiet*."

That makes Julia smile. "I know, bruh," she says. Then she rubs her bottom lip hard and looks at my carpet. "Sorry."

"That's okay, *bruh*," I say, grinning at her.

Julia comes over and sits on the bed next to me and Isabella. She pulls her hair back tight, like she is trying to pull it out or something, but then she lets it fall around her shoulders in a thick black curtain. There's no trace of highlights. She touches my armband. "You were really brave."

I shake off her words. Maybe if I really had been brave, I would've told Julia a long time ago how her ditching us made me feel.

"I *really* missed you," I say. "A lot." I look at our pictures on my bulletin board. It's like three different girls. "But what you said is true," I say. "Things change. *People* change."

Julia nods and gives my shoulder a nudge with hers. "The command thing with Tyler was mean," she says low, and starts blinking fast.

"Yeah, it was," I can't help saying.

"For a minute it was"—Julia lets her hair fall in her face—"sort of fun to be mean?" She peeks at me through her hair. "I know that sounds awful," she adds really fast.

"I don't know how being mean could be fun," Isabella says.

"Seriously," I say.

"I guess what I meant was . . ." Julia pauses to figure it out. "Stacy has a ton of friends, so it was nice feeling popular too."

"So you have to be mean to be popular?" Isabella asks incredulously.

"No, you don't," I say.

"Sort of," Julia says. But then she adds, "It didn't feel like being mean as much as it felt like being funny. And I swear I didn't think you and Tyler would really end up kissing."

"Well, he sure shouldn't have gone along with it. But I wish you would've told Stacy not to play a joke on me."

Julia nods. "I should've. I knew it was messed up. It can be hard to stand up to Stacy sometimes. But I shouldn't have gone along with something I knew wasn't right."

"Unless you get commanded," Isabella says, and she sounds so serious, it takes me a second to realize she's joking.

Julia smiles. "Yeah, except then." She holds up her hands, showing her uncrossed fingers, and it's like she's daring us.

I want to shout, "Command!" and tell Julia she has to stay best friends with us. But any friendship manual would tell you that's not the way to keep a friend.

"So . . . what now?" Isabella asks.

"I guess I just wanted to know if . . ." Julia licks her lips. "If I'm still a part of the United Nations?"

"Of course you are!" Isabella says.

"Always," I say.

Julia pinches the bridge of her nose and takes what our fifth-grade teacher called a cleansing breath. I figure it can't hurt, and take one too.

I hold out my phone so we can all fit into the selfie. With our heads pressed close together and our smiles as wide as the sky, we look completely united.

Sometimes you don't even realize you're holding your breath until you finally let it out.

70
New Path

The next day at lunch, I get a great idea. It is an itchy-palm idea, but I can't always worry about my hands. After all I went through with the armbands, I don't want everything to just stay the same at school. It's time for a change.

I stand up.

"Come on, let's go!" I say to my friends. Although I understand everything Julia said yesterday, I'm still glad to have the United Nations together again. United.

"What?" Isabella asks. "Where?"

"Don't worry about that," I say. "Just come on."

Julia zips up her lunch bag. "Fine." She stands up.

I stop at the table where Julia's other friends are. "Get up, everyone!" I tell them. "Come on."

Stacy giggles and gets right up. In that moment, I can see what Julia meant about her. That's one girl who is always going to be up for anything. Lynn sort of shakes her head but gets up too. And then everyone else gets up and follows me to the basketball courts. I figure there's no reason we can't all be united.

When we get there, everyone is cool and like, "Hey, how's it going?" We are all wearing armbands, and I feel really proud about that.

Bernard grimaces at me, which is really him smiling, and I smile big back.

On the other side of Bernard is Yolanda. And on the other side of her is Tyler. They're holding hands, and she is cheesing that upside-down Y like she just won a huge prize. I don't know how I missed how big she was crushing on him.

The sun feels great on my face. Seeing the United Nations get a whole lot bigger feels awesome. I lean over and give Bernard a nudge.

"Hey, Bernard," I say. "Do you think we could ask Mr. Levy for us to be lab partners again?"

He gives me a high five so hard, I have to rub my hand on my pants.

"Ow!" I say, laughing.

Bernard's laughter is so loud, it's like a lion's roar.

71
Pages & Pages

That night, I pull out my eyeball journal. It's gotten a little ratty over the course of the year.

I flip through the journal, looking over the things I wrote. Some of them are pages and pages long, but most of them are short and to the point.

Green eyes are hot!

Cafeteria lunches are nasty.

As I'm reading, Hana comes strolling into my room. Without knocking.

"You're almost an eighth grader. You must think you're all that."

She joins me on my bed, close enough that our arms

touch. The armband on my left arm touching the one on her right.

"Is eighth going to be easier?" I ask.

"Oh, yeah, it's all chill after seventh," she jokes, but then she gets serious. "Hey, good job with the armbands."

I look at her. "But it's not really going to change anything."

"Change is hard." She shrugs. "But that doesn't mean we stop, right?"

"Right."

"Besides," she says, "seems like it changed *you*. And that's pretty important."

She gets up, and as she leaves, she holds her fist up and so I hold mine up too. And then she walks out . . . leaving the door open, of course.

I get up, shut the door, and go back to reading my journal. I went through a lot this year.

I wonder what pages I should paper-clip together so Ms. Jacobs doesn't read them. There are a *lot* of embarrassing entries.

I decide not to clip any.

Maybe Emerson was right when he talked about learning through suffering. I mean, this year wasn't easy, but I sure learned a lot.

I look at the piece of paper I tacked up with the quote Daddy and Hana told me. The James Baldwin one about not being able to change anything unless you face it. I may not have changed much, but I sure learned something important.

I make one final entry.

Some things are worth the trouble. For real.

Acknowledgments

The time between writing this book and getting it published was long. I mean, looooong. I couldn't have kept going without the love and support of my husband, Keith, and my kids: Morgan and Jordan. My loves. My heart. My husband has *always* supported me on this journey. He cheered me on and never once said I should maybe stop trying, even after years of rejections. And my kids? Shoot. They just always knew I was going to get a book published. They'd tell their friends their mama was a writer and that was it. And I have to give a special shout-out to Morgan, who read so many variations of this book and loved it (at least so she said) every time.

My critique partner, Jenn Kompos, is the realest, most wonderful person, and I'm so blessed to have met her at an SCBWI conference years ago. Not only is her input always on point, it always, always makes my writing better. This book wouldn't exist without her and all the times she made me dig deeper and find Shayla's voice.

So much gratitude for my agent, Brenda Bowen, who called me to say she wanted to introduce Shayla to the world and in that first conversation talked about me *holding my book in my hands*. And then she went to work to make my dream come true. My editor, Alessandra Balzer, who is no joke and won't let anything slide, but has the kindest way of letting me know when my work should be a bit more "nuanced." I love the Balzer + Bray corner of HarperCollins we get to live in. Thank you to all the folks at HarperCollins who worked so hard to get this book out into the world: Kelsey Murphy, Renée Cafiero, Alison Donalty, Robby Imfeld, Ann Dye, Nellie Kurtzman, Patty Rosati, Molly Motch, Kathy Faber, Andrea Pappenheimer, and Kerry Moynagh. And my goodness, artist Alleanna Harris and designer Aurora Parlagreco, who gave me such a gorgeous cover? Goose bumps every time!

Thank you to my sensitivity readers for giving me

such great input. Any mistakes with cultural representation are mine and mine alone.

Special shout-out to Jazz, who shared some middle school lingo (but if I got any of that wrong, it is totally my fault).

Mamasita Baunita. There's just no me without you. My mom is the best. You think yours is, but mine really is. My sisters, Pamela and Linda—we are the Black Brontë sisters—and brother Jimmy: storytellers all. So much better than me. The "in-laws" who are *truly* blood. Marriages gave me fantastic sisters and some pretty cool brothers. Honestly, I'm fortunate to have such a wide, boisterous, loving family, and to all my aunts, uncles, cousins (especially Rach, who told me over and over to believe until I did), nieces, and nephews, you are overbrimming with love and stories. I owe you all the biggest most heartfelt thank-you.

My BFFs (no, seriously, FOREVER): Marisa, Alane, and Griff. Don't tell anyone my secrets, okay? I love you; you each have taught me what real friendship looks like.

My SOTYs, sisters for life: Kim, Kelli, Dawn, Lisa, Lisa, and Marisa. What can I even say? You're my life support and obviously inspired the book club scene. My critique group—the Panama Math & Science Club. (Don't ask.) Such a great group of writers who love and support each other. Lydia, Sally, Kath, Stacy, and Rose—we make such an awesome team! Can't wait for the world to read your books. The NorCal writing community that I've become part of, and especially Misa, Kelly, Randy, Sabaa, Stephanie, Stacey, and Lindsay. My coworkers at SU who got to go on the best part of this journey with me and have supported me throughout.

I have a particular fondness for contests, as I gained so much from them. Pitch Madness gave me hope (#Teambowserscastle forever!); #DVpit showed me there was interest in Shayla's story; WCNV helped me write a fantastic query; and PitchWars gave me such a wonderful writing community. They cheered every request and supported every pass, and if there was room here, I'd thank each and every one of them. Special love to Brenda, of course; Tabitha! And Kit, Tomi, and Adalyn, who were so generous with their time and answered questions, offering support and advice; and my sister-in-arms, Gwynne, who is going to get her shot.

My first publishing girls: Robyn, Nancy, and Virginia—you gave me so much confidence way back in the day, and I'm forever grateful. Speaking of Disney . . . Nikki Grimes, thank you for calling me a writer before anybody else did.

Thanks to Terrie, for listening and always, always being there; Trudy, for maybe being happier about this book selling than I was; Donna, for all the miles we've logged together; Keely, for hours on the phone and tarot readings; Karen, for letting me keep it real—it's so cool being on this journey with you; the always-encouraging Carol, Lori and Sue, and my Zumberas, who have truly kept me sane for all these years (especially Gertrude, Mimi, Judith, and Anne, who are more than Zumberas but also the most wonderfulest of friends).

Thank you to Jacqueline Woodson, who wished me luck the day I went on sub (it worked!); Jason Reynolds, who welcomed me into the writers' club when I was just a chick with a book deal and he was . . . Jason Reynolds; Angie Thomas, who maybe will never know how much it meant when she told me she liked my book; Erin Entrada Kelly (who let me fangirl all over her) and Jay Coles who are not only inspirations but also blew my mind by agreeing to read the book and said such amazingly kind things; Tim Federle, who gave me direction at a pivotal moment; Adam Silvera, who inspired me to expand Mr. Powell's role; Dhonielle Clayton, Corey Ann Haydu, Nic Stone, and countless other authors who inspire and encourage me. And thank you to Angela at Kepler's, who didn't laugh when I told her I'd hold a signing at her bookstore one day and has cheered me on before there was anything to celebrate.

We need diverse books, Black girl magic is real, and Black lives matter.